W9-AGQ-191

Morocco Community Library
205 S. West Street
P O Box 87
Morocco, IN 47963

Diamond Beanies

Tres Bon Chronicle Series Volume Two

By Dennis O. Hendry

Edited by Vivienne A. Thibodeaux

[i]

Text copyright © 2013 by Dennis O. Hendry

All Rights Reserved

This is a work of fiction. Names, characters, places, and incidents either are the product of the author's imagination or are used fictitiously. Any resemblance to actual persons, living or dead, events, or locales is entirely coincidental.

ISBN: 978-0-9894697-3-9

NCPL
Morocco Community Library
205 S. West Street
For Grandma Ida   P O Box 87
Morocco, IN 47963

Edward's quest for the Roman Denarius tribute penny, the Biblical coin that was once in the hands of Jesus of Nazareth, leads him to the hometown of a distant relative in America. Unable to escape their fate, Edward and Elisabeth find themselves helplessly drawn into an adventure full of unexpected revelations that reignites the worldwide phenomenon of the legendary and adorable beanie bears.

From the creator of the *Tres Bon Chronicles* comes the anticipated sequel, *Diamond Beanies*, where Indiana's historic Grande Kankakee River and a charming small Midwestern town provide the inviting locations for the next wondrous journey; one filled with remembrance and honor, conflicts and challenges, and a grandmother's poignant lesson of faith, hope, and charity.

[iii]

TABLE OF CONTENTS

Chapter 1 Flight

"Flight now boarding," a pleasant, female voice called.

"Hey Elisabeth, it's time to get to the check in station," Edward said.

Elisabeth zipped up her purse; the one Edward had been making fun of the whole time they had been in the airport. He thought it was too funny. She had an extra-large purse. He called it luggage. But Elisabeth was so happy with the new purse she got in London, that she didn't care what he called it, she liked it. Besides, it seemed she always had something Edward needed in there.

"Flight now boarding," the attendant called over the loud speaker.

"Let's go," Edward said. "We need to board."

They gathered up their things, handed the attendant their boarding passes, and took their seats. The flight was full, and the crew seemed very nice and helpful. After they stored their things in the overhead bins, Edward took a seat by the window.

"Welcome aboard all. This is a flight to John F. Kennedy International Airport in New York, and we have clearance for takeoff. Please buckle your seatbelts and prepare for takeoff."

Elisabeth was ready to get home, and Edward was anxious to see them continue the adventure into his family's past in the new world, America. The flight left the runway in normal fashion, and cruised to altitude for the flight over the Atlantic.

The crew was busy serving some light meals and refreshments when the pilot's voice came over from the cabin, and asked the crew and passengers to stay seated and buckled up in case they experienced some mild turbulence. The pilot routed the aircraft away from some cloud formations they were seeing on the radar. The other flights ahead of them had reported a storm up ahead.

Just as Edward was pouring his drink, the plane suddenly listed to the starboard side, and seemed to lose a lot of altitude. The sound of the passengers gasping was unmistakable as the engines roared to peak level. The plane seemed to stabilize, but everyone stayed tense. The crew calmed themselves, and continued to serve the passengers.

"Wow, that was not fun," Elisabeth said.

"Oh, it wasn't that bad. I have flown in a lot of small puddle jumpers in my day and those are a lot worse," Edward replied.

The flight continued, but Edward couldn't help but think that after the mishap, the engines didn't sound the same. He shrugged it off as no big deal because the rest of the flight went well and they landed safely.

The pilot came on over the speakers while they were taxiing to thank them for choosing the airline and taking the mishap in stride. He said their calmness was very much appreciated.

The plane taxied to the gate as Edward was removing his bag from the overhead. The bag turned over, and a small figurine fell out onto the seat. Elisabeth saw it, picked it up, and gave it to Edward.

"Here, I think this fell out of your bag. Is this yours?" she asked.

"Oh yes, thank you so much, it is an old family heirloom I have. I carry it wherever I go."

"Oh yeah, it's really neat. Is it a wooden lamb? It looks really old."

"Yes, it is really old. My grandpa told me it dates back centuries."

"It's our turn in the aisle," Elisabeth said and nudged Edward.

As they made their way down the aisle, they came to the door where the pilot and the co-pilot were talking to the ground maintenance crew. They seemed very concerned and the flight attendant was trying to block the view of them, but Edward heard them talking.

"Well, we don't know how you did it, but we have never seen anything like that before," the maintenance guy said.

"How bad is it?" the co-pilot asked.

"Real bad, the aileron actuator was completely nonfunctional," the maintenance guy said.

"She seemed heavy, but she kept flying straight. It felt strange, and I thought something was amiss, but it kept flying. The systems were in check, so we just kept the throttle up, and made sure everything was fine," the pilot said.

"I have never seen this happen to a plane that still makes it to its destination after the misalignment of the actuators. The system should have been lighting up every warning light on your panel," the maintenance guy said.

"Well, it's a good thing it didn't because we had nowhere to go! We were in the middle of the Atlantic! We would have had to ditch and hope for the best," the pilot said.

"Yes, you would have had to ditch with a problem like this. The only other time I have heard of this, was a plane flying over Iowa. They landed immediately and barely made it. It wasn't pretty, but they survived. This plane needs some major work, so we will have to ground it for quite a while," the maintenance guy said.

5

"Alright then, let's just chalk this one up as someone watching over us," the co-pilot said.

"Yeah, you were either lucky or had a guiding hand to help you."

"Edward, did you hear that? Our plane barely made it! We are really lucky to be here," Elisabeth said.

"Yes, Elisabeth, that was really crazy. We could have been a news story of a lost plane over the Atlantic, but something made sure we made it home," Edward said as he put the wooden lamb in his pocket.

They got through the airport and collected their bags at the carousel.

"Are you sure you want to drive back to Indiana instead of flying?" Elisabeth asked.

"Yes, I want to soak up all I can while I am here," Edward said.

"It probably is for the best since the last flight was quirky," she said.

They made their way over to the rental car kiosks and checked in for a car.

"How is this for cool?" Elisabeth asked. "We got upgraded to a Cadillac touring sedan! This is so cool! We are going in style now!" she beamed.

They walked across the rental lot and found a beautiful, new, garnet red touring sedan.

"Wow, this is really nice. It's huge!" Edward said.

"Yes, it sure is nice. You are going to like riding in this all the way back."

Elisabeth hit the trunk button on the remote and they loaded their luggage in. She slid into the driver's seat and took a deep breath. The car smelled brand new.

"Got to love the smell of new leather seats," Edward said.

"Yeah, brand new leather seats. It reminds me of my dad's car. This is going to be so much fun," Elisabeth said.

7

They drove to the exit gate and the on-ramp to the interstate. Elisabeth paddle shifted through the gears for fun and accelerated through the traffic.

"Follow the signs to the west," Edward said.

"Keep an eye out so I don't miss the exit," Elisabeth said.

"Will do. Hey wait, what is this? It says 'screen' on it."

"Push it!" she said.

Edward pushed the button and a screen rose up out of the dashboard. "This is great! It's a navigation screen to help us get where we want to go," Edward said.

"Put in LaPorte, Indiana. That should keep us on the right track."

Edward typed in the destination and sure enough, it showed their current GPS location, and the best route to get out of town and head west.

"Good thing we have this or we might have gotten lost in that last spaghetti bowl back there. Who knows where we would have ended up?" Edward said.

"Yes, this will make life a lot easier," Elisabeth said.

The interstate seemed endless, and each long stretch seemed to wander into the next.

"So this is Ohio?" Edward asked.

"Yeah, it won't be long now. I had better call my mom to check in."

Elisabeth swiped her phone and pressed the home icon.

"Hi Mom, it's me! Yes, we are fine. We are almost leaving Ohio, so it won't be long. Edward needs to know if he should call ahead to reserve a hotel room to stay in. Oh, really? Yes, I will ask him."

Elisabeth turned to Edward and asked if he would like to stay at Grandma Ida's house if he didn't think it was too weird.

"That would be great," Edward said. "It might give me some hints about where I need to look for the treasure."

"I am sure there may be something there for you to get some direction," Elisabeth said.

Elisabeth put the phone back to her ear. "Yes, Mom, he said he is ok with it, so we will see you in a few hours. Yes, I will drive safe and I will call you when we get closer. Bye, bye."

It didn't take long for the Cadillac to chew up the miles. Before they knew it, they were rolling down the off ramp of the toll road.

Chapter 2 Home

"Wow, this is so cool. We are here already," Edward said. "This town is so quaint. It's exactly how I pictured it would be."

"We need to stop at my house first to get the keys to my grandma's house."

Elisabeth turned at the stoplight on the west edge of town and onto a road. It was an old, county road that led them to the subdivision. It wasn't a brand new subdivision, but it looked to be newer than the ones they passed in town. The houses were just a little more upscale then the other houses and she drove right up to a yellow shuttered Cape Cod style home.

"Well, here we are," she said.

"Oh, it sure is nice, Elisabeth."

"My mom wanted to move out of town, but not into anything too large, just something she could enjoy, and still have some space."

"It looks like she picked a good one. It reminds me of the hillside homes in southern France."

"Yes, it kind of does, now that you mention it."

As they pulled up the driveway, Trinity opened the front door to greet them.

"I am sure glad to see you both made it safe and intact. I hope you got along well. I see the weather was fine. What did you think of her driving, Edward? I hope she was on her best behavior for you," Trinity said, like a mom who was always watching over her kids no matter how old they were.

"Mom, I was a good driver, and Edward was too. He said it was strange driving on the other side of the road, but after a while he felt ok, and we made it here just fine," Elisabeth said.

"Oh good, well let's go inside and get you two something to eat. You must be starving and ready to get out of that car by now," Trinity said.

"I would like to eat something and then just sit on the couch," Elisabeth said.

Trinity got their things out of the trunk and walked them into the house.

"It sure is good to be home," Elisabeth said as she entered the living room.

Edward took a look around. "This is nice. It's very warm and welcoming. Now I see why you like to be home." He sat on the couch and sunk in comfortably. "Ah, it feels good to be out of the car. Driving is fun and all, but your brain never shuts off. There's so much to see and pay attention to. It's not as bad as England, but the lack of a change of scenery can sure lull you to sleep. It's beautiful here, but the miles and miles of corn just makes you feel like you are flying low instead of driving," he smirked.

"You do get to see a lot of farm ground, but it is a true testament to how we can feed the world," Trinity said.

"You said it. That is what I was thinking. All these crops are food for someone, and it's incredibly bountiful," Edward said.

"You two are making me hungry. What do you have to eat, Mom? Something smells good around here," Elisabeth said.

"Yes, dear, I made some sweet corn and some ribs. They should be perfect by now."

"Let's eat then!" Edward said.

The meal was superb and the conversation flew by in an instant. As they finished up their dessert, Edward thanked Trinity for her offer to let him stay at Ida's.

"Are you sure it would be ok? I can get a hotel room somewhere," Edward said.

"Mom, I think he should stay at Grandma's. It's empty and it would help him get a sense of her. We will feel secure knowing that someone is watching over the place."

"The house is empty and since the obituary announcement was in the paper, I have been worrying about it being broken into," Trinity said. "Please stay there, I insist."

"Yes, ok, that would be wonderful," Edward said. "I would be happy to stay over there to watch over the place."

"Thank you, Edward. Now, that's settled," Trinity said.

14

"Let's go then, I will take you there. We will make sure everything is on and working," Elisabeth said.

Edward thanked Trinity for the delicious meal, and he and Elisabeth headed for the car.

Chapter 3 Tulips

Elisabeth and Edward headed out to go over to Ida's house. As they pulled up to the house, Edward could feel the aura of Ida even before they reached the driveway. It was a sense of home, a sense of security of being welcomed. The house was just like he pictured it, a small bungalow with pretty shutters, and a well-kept lawn. Her house had been well cared for, and had aged gracefully.

"Well, here we are," Elisabeth said. "But from the look on your face you already know, don't you?"

"Yes, it looks really comforting," Edward said.

The driveway was gravel, and the sound of the rocks under the tires seemed to sing a welcoming tune. Elisabeth felt like she had just been here moments before, seeing Ida in the front window. They gathered Edward's things out of the trunk and walked up the well-worn sidewalk to the front porch. Edward suddenly stopped at the bottom of the first step.

"Oh my," he said.

"What?" Elisabeth asked.

"These tulips are beautiful," he said.

"Yes, they are quite gorgeous."

"You don't see their importance?"

"No, why?" Elisabeth asked.

"They are green with blue highlights! I haven't seen tulips like these since I've been to my grandmother's house. I remember seeing them each time I went to visit, but never paid a moment's notice until one day I was on a tour of the royal garden in England when it was in full bloom."

Edward sat down on the porch step and continued his story.

"I asked the tour guide about the tulips and if they had any green ones with blue variations. She gave me the strangest look and turned away in haste. I wondered the whole rest of the tour what the big deal was. When the tour ended and everyone left, I went over to her. I was going to

18

apologize for whatever it was I said when she interrupted me, and took me by the arm. She led me through a stone gate to a garden surrounded by giant hedge row. As soon as I turned the corner I saw them, the same green tulips with blue highlights on them. They were the best cared for tulips I had ever seen. She asked me how I knew about them, so I told her I had seen some before. She was quite surprised, and told me that was impossible, as those were the only ones existing today. I didn't want to argue with her, so I told her I must have been mistaken. Then she showed me the way to the exit. I had a strange feeling all the way home. It felt like someone was following me, but I could never put my finger on it."

"Why didn't you tell her about your grandma's tulips?" Elisabeth asked.

"Well, I just had a weird feeling there was more to the story, and I wanted to do some more research into it first," Edward said.

"Are these the same tulips your grandmother had, and the same as the ones in the royal garden?"

"Yes, they are exactly the same!" Edward said. "Why don't we go inside, so I can pull up some information on the Internet to show you?"

"Ok, I think the Internet is still on here. The computer is newer, so it should do fine," Elisabeth said.

Elisabeth unlocked the door and they entered the foyer. It brought a sense of warmth that Elisabeth easily remembered. When she looked over at Edward, his expression said he was filled with the very same warmth. The house exuded a comforting feeling, like a warm blanket right out of the dryer. They both knew Ida was with them, and her aura was watching over them.

"It's over here," Elisabeth said as she pointed to the sitting room off the foyer.

"Oh wow, is this her computer?" Edward asked.

"Yes, I was with her the day she bought it," Elisabeth said. "Why?"

"It's so up to date. This is one powerful desktop for your grandma to have."

"Well, she wanted something good, so we let her get what she wanted."

"Good job there, Elisabeth," Edward said, as he pushed the power buttons on the router, the tower, and the monitor. "Let's see how fast this thing is."

The router began blinking and connected to the Internet right away. All the connection lights turned steady and the computer whirred to life.

"It looks like it's working," Edward said.

"Yes, it always worked really well," Elisabeth said. "I always thought it was fast. It is a lot faster than mine," she smiled.

The computer ran through its startup and the system came up. Edward clicked on the browser and logged into a search engine.

"Let's see," he said. "Where is the quickest place to go to show you the tulips?"

"How about wiki?" Elisabeth asked.

"Yes, that would be the fastest," Edward said. He typed 'tulips wiki' and the search engine quickly returned the link. He clicked the link, and brought up a page full of information on tulips.

"You see here, it says all about tulips and their existence in areas surrounding Israel. They were found in the wild since some very early times. The tulips are all different types, but there is no mention of a green and blue tulip. The only thing I have ever found is a reference to tulips around Judea and Persia during Biblical days. It was a rare flower of its time, but the existence of the exact green and blue tulip is something I have never documented," Edward said.

"My grandma has had these tulips ever since I can remember. They seem to stay in bloom longer than any other flower she has. Every time I come here, they are blooming. She used to spend a lot of time taking care of them quite diligently. I never really paid that much attention to them. Thanks for telling me. I will keep my eyes open to see if I can find out about their origin," Elisabeth said.

"I would appreciate that a lot. Any help you can give would go a long way in finding out why the royal gardener was so interested in them. But please keep this between us. You know, it's weird, but the feeling I was getting from the gardener was very strange, and not good either, if you know what I mean."

"I will keep this between us, Edward, and if I see or find anything, I will tell you in confidence."

"Thanks," Edward said.

"Here, let me show you where the guest bedroom is. I really liked coming to stay over here because she kept the room so nice and peaceful. I would always get my best sleep here," Elisabeth said.

They walked down the hallway and past Ida's room. Edward stopped momentarily to look in. He got a sense of solace, and he somehow knew he was welcome here, because Ida's room exuded a familiar sense. It was the same feeling he used to get when he was at his dad's grandmother's house.

They entered the guest bedroom. "Here is a dresser for you to put your things in while you are here. The linens and towels are in the hallway closet for you to use. There is a spare house key on the hook next to the back door. You can use that while you are here, too," Elisabeth said. "I will come over tomorrow to see what you want to do."

"Not too early," Edward said. "You know it's been a long few days, and I want to sleep in. I think I will sleep quite well here," he grinned.

"Oh yes, you probably will," Elisabeth replied. "Good night."

Elisabeth headed down the hallway and through the front door. She turned off the lights on her way out. Edward heard her car pull out of the driveway. He laid down to rest in his new found, peaceful place. It wasn't long before he was sleeping deeply, and the quiet neighborhood sounds drifted away into the night.

Chapter 4 Trunk

Edward awoke to a small peek of sunshine coming through the door frame. He lay in bed relishing the moment of waking at Ida's house. The house had a quaint calmness to it that reminded him so much of his own grandma's house. He smiled, and folded his hands together remembering his grandma.

It was only moments after he had cleaned up and walked into the kitchen, when the doorbell rang. He looked out and saw Elisabeth's car in the drive. "Oh good, perfect timing," he thought, as he rushed to the front door to greet her.

"Good morning!" he beamed.

"Well, good morning to you!" Elisabeth said. "You look rested and ready to take on the world."

"Yes, I feel great. I am ready for adventure."

"Well, alright then, let's start with a treasure hunt in the attic," Elisabeth said.

They went down the hall to the attic door, and up the old, wooden stairs. Elisabeth pulled the cord to turn on the lights. There were boxes neatly stored there, with only one path all the way down the middle of the room. The scent of vintage cardboard lingered in the air. Elisabeth pulled one box off the top and opened it. Inside there were numerous doilies of very fine quality. Each one was unique.

"Aren't these really nice?" Elisabeth said. She held one up for Edward to see.

"Yeah, they look exactly like my grandma's. She used to have a collection just like it."

Edward moved some boxes to the aisle, and began to make another path to the back of the attic. Just as he moved a large box over to the side, he caught a glimpse of a wooden trunk that was hiding behind the other boxes.

"Hey, look over here!" he said. He pushed the boxes quickly out of the way.

"Wow, look at that!" Elisabeth said.

"It's huge!" Edward said.

It was an old, wooden trunk, with a metal frame around it.

"This looks really old. The wood is worn from years of storage. I have only seen something like this in an old family photo taken at my great grandpa's," Edward said.

"Yes, it is too cool! I would have never guessed my grandma would have something like this, and not have it downstairs on display. It is truly a treasure. I wonder what's in it."

"I don't know, but it must be important because it was stashed away deep, for some reason. Let's take a look."

They tried to open the trunk. "I can't get it open," Edward said. "It's locked and it would be nearly impossible to break into it."

Just then the telephone rang. It was the typical, old, bell ringer, and it echoed loudly throughout the house.

"Hey, it's the phone," Edward said.

"Oh yeah, it is the phone. I thought it was the fire alarm," Elisabeth said. "I forgot Grandma had that old phone. I could never get used to that noise. Only serious alarms have that loud of a bell," she said.

"I kind of miss the old bell ringers," Edward retorted. The phone rang some more and it seemed to be echoing louder.

"We had better hurry and get it before the answering machine picks up," Elisabeth said.

"Oh, it will be alright," Edward replied. "I am sure your grandma doesn't have an answering machine."

"You would be surprised by my grandma!" Elisabeth snipped.

Elisabeth rushed down the stairs, and they creaked out their old, dried out wood harmony.

"Hello," she said out of breath. "Yes, Mom, we were just checking out some things around the house."

"Would you get Edward and grab the keys to your grandma's car and meet me for brunch?" Trinity asked on the other end.

"That would be great. We will be right over." Elisabeth hung up and went to get Edward.

"Edward! My mom wants to meet for brunch. I presume you are hungry?" Elisabeth asked.

"You bet I am. I could use some real non-homogenized, non-commercial food."

"Good, she wants to meet at the family restaurant downtown. We need Grandma's car keys. I think they are on a hook behind this kitchen closet door. Yes, here they are."

"Did you happen to find a funny looking key for the trunk?" Edward asked.

"No, but I did look. You must have read my mind."

"I knew you were still thinking about the trunk, because I am too," Edward said. "Well, let's go, I can drive."

They reached the restaurant, and found Trinity waiting for them outside.

"Well hello, you two. I hope you are keeping your grandma's house in order," Trinity said.

"Yes, Mom, everything's fine," Elisabeth said.

They ate a hearty lunch and enjoyed the company with Edward. The time flew by quickly. Trinity looked at her watch to see it was almost twelve thirty. "Oh dear, look at the time. I need to get to my hair appointment," Trinity said.

"I don't want to be too forward, but do you think I could use Ida's car to go check out some sights?" Edward asked.

"Of course, Edward, that would be fine," Trinity said. "I will take Elisabeth back to the house so she can pick up her car, and I can still make it to my hair stylist in time."

"Thanks!" Edward said. "If I have any trouble, I can call Elisabeth on her cell."

"You should be fine, just drive safely," Trinity said.

Edward took off in Ida's car to do some exploring on his own. Trinity and Elisabeth agreed to meet up with him later on.

Chapter 5 Bank

Elisabeth got into her car and drove downtown. She remembered she needed to stop at the bank to make a deposit. The bank was nearly empty as she was filling out her paperwork. She thought back to the trunk at her grandma's house.

"No, it couldn't be," she thought. "But maybe it could. Would she have left the key in the safe deposit box, or at least a clue? It would be just about par for her to do something like that. Well, I am here, so I might as well check it again. It couldn't hurt."

Elisabeth went over to the receptionist and asked if she could check her safe deposit box.

"Yes, just sign in here and see the attendant. She will help you with the box," the receptionist said.

"Thank you," Elisabeth said. She signed in and walked over to the desk where the attendant was waiting and took a seat in the chair. The attendant asked for her identification, which Elisabeth handed to her, and the attendant keyed the information in the terminal. It beeped twice and a screen popped up.

"Hmm, this is not normal," the attendant said.

"What is it?" Elisabeth asked.

"The system says you're connected to two boxes."

"What? I only have one box," Elisabeth said.

"Let me check again. This is a new system, and we just had all the records imported into it, so maybe it's a cross reference mistake."

"It must be. I only have one key, and it opened up the box the last time I was here."

"Yes, I see that. You were here a few months ago," the attendant said. She typed some information into another screen, and it beeped twice again. "It still says you have two boxes. They were both originally opened by the same person, on the same day, years ago."

"That seems like a keying error," Elisabeth said.

"I think so too, but it won't hurt to go check it out and see if there really are two boxes. We can see if the one key fits both of them," the attendant said.

"Yes, let's go look," Elisabeth said.

They made their way into the vault and the attendant pulled out the first box.

"That's the one I accessed a few months ago," Elisabeth said.

The attendant pulled out another box. "This is the other one," she said. "Let's go put them down in the viewing cubicle to see if the key you have fits."

They went to the cubicle, and the attendant put down the second box. She placed her key in the lock, and Elisabeth placed her key into the other.

"Well, let's see if this works," the attendant said.

They both turned their keys, and with the sound of a click, the lock popped open. The look on both their faces was sheer disbelief.

"It looks like the system was right after all. I will leave you alone to conduct your business. I will make a note in the system to correlate the one key for the two boxes," the attendant said, and she turned to leave.

"Thank you so much," Elisabeth said.

Elisabeth was very curious and quite set aback. She slowly opened the box. "Who knows what Grandma Ida has in store for me now," she thought.

She opened the box and found a manila envelope inside. It was sealed, but had handwriting on the outside that said '*Have fun with this adventure!*' There was a smiley face drawn next to it. It was in Ida's handwriting. Elisabeth knew right away it was her grandma's writing.

She took the envelope and slowly opened the top. Inside were several sheets of paper. She carefully took them out and laid them on the desk.

"Oh my," she thought. "Wow!" she said out loud. "I can't believe it!"

The note was on a piece of pastel pink stationary, with more pastel colored paisleys on the left side of the border. There were green, red, and yellow pastel butterflies across the top.

"This is the stationary I gave her when I was seven. I gave it to her for Mother's Day," Elisabeth thought.

She recalled the day she bought it, when she was with her mom at the store. It was a pleasant, early spring day. She was just shopping with her mom and happened to walk down the arts and crafts aisle. Even though it was tucked away down low in the back of the shelf, it stuck out to her like a sore thumb. She was drawn to the pretty stationary. She knew right away she had to buy it for her grandma.

"Well, I am not sure we need that," Trinity said that day.

"Oh Mom, please, it's so pretty! I want to give it to Grandma!" she pleaded.

"Ok, ok," her mom said grudgingly. "But only if you save it for Mother's Day in a few weeks. That would make her very happy that you got her something."

"Yes, Mom."

Elisabeth remembered how great that all was, because Grandma sometimes seemed sad on Mother's Day, and her gift would make it so much better for her. That day seemed like yesterday for Elisabeth, and she recognized the stationary immediately. Oh, it was a wonderful memory, one she was so happy to have back. It seemed like a special time that only came around once in a while.

She picked up the paper and read the note.

I hope this discovery finds you well. I have a special mission set out for you, and it would be swell if you chose to take it on. This adventure should be taken with great care as it is intended to be fun, and a once in a lifetime experience. It is not to be used for ill-gotten gains, and is best suited to be a shared experience with all who have the chance to enjoy it.

38

The following pages contain a list of two hundred beanie babies, their name, and type. The two hundred chosen can be uniquely identified in a number of ways. I have done my best to make sure they are unique and original. I have taken great care to make sure they cannot be copied or imitated. I have given you the following markers that you must find to authenticate these beanies, and begin the journey that all must enjoy. This journey will most likely take on a life of its own, so embrace the mission, and keep a level head.

I have left three of these original beanies in the box for you to do with as you wish. I hope you find them well. The locations of the first markers that inventory each unique beanie are in a large trunk, which I last left in the attic of my house. It can be readily opened with a special locket of a unique shape that acts like a key. The locket was a very special gift from my great-great grandmother, and was always meant to be the key to the trunk. In the trunk, you will find more of the unique beanies. They will help you on your journey ahead.

I always lived with a giddy feeling that someday when I left this earth, someone would

have the chance to have an adventure, and a
wondrous time doing so. Make the best of it, and
remember that life is something to be treasured
throughout its journey, and the ongoing adventure
should be left for others to enjoy.

Your friend in life, Ida

Elisabeth was barely able to comprehend
the gravity of it all. She reached into the box,
pulled out the three beanies, and closed the box.
She pushed the attendant bell, and waited
patiently. She tried to grasp the situation she was
in.

"What should I do now?" she thought. "Do
I get my mom, or Edward, or both, or tell no one,
and go over to check out the trunk alone?"

No, that was not what Ida would have
wanted her to do. She needed them to help her.
She heard the bell ring and the attendant was
outside the booth now. She had forgotten all about
putting the box back.

"May I help you?" the attendant asked.

"Oh, yes, I am ready to put the box back now."

"Sure, let's put it back then."

They took the box and slipped it into its respective location, and keyed the lock closed. As they walked out of the vault, the attendant posed a question to Elisabeth.

"I usually don't pry, but I have to ask," she said. "I see you have some beanie bears. Normally, I wouldn't give it a second thought, but you see when the beanie baby was at its height of being collected, I must have had a hundred or so of them. I have since gotten rid of most of them, except for a few I just had to keep for memory's sake. I see the one you have is a special limited edition bear. I haven't seen one of those in years. I remember when it came out, I went all over to find one, but never could get one. I was always just one step too late in getting into the store. Boy, people would stake out stores and wait for deliveries."

"Oh, really?" Elisabeth asked.

"Yes, that one was my nemesis. I could never afford to buy one. When I checked on eBay,

41

the price was always too high. Then the bottom fell out and I lost interest. But I see you have one."

"Yes, my grandma left it in the box for me. Isn't it nice?"

"Oh yes, it is very nice."

"Well, if you promise me one thing, I will let you have it."

"Anything, anything at all!"

"If you promise to never sell it, and always keep it safe, you are welcome to have this one."

"Really? That's easy! I can promise you I will never sell it, because it's more valuable to me then it will ever be worth to someone else. I don't think the market will come around like it was back then. It's like the tulip bubble in the Dutch Golden Age. I started researching that for a class I had. Everyone wanted a tulip, but when there were enough to go around, they lost their value, and their value never returned. Just like a true bubble, when something is readily available, the price seeks its own normal level, even in the midst of hysteria," the attendant said.

42

"The tulip bubble? What's that?" Elisabeth asked.

"Oh you might not have heard of it," the attendant said. "Let me explain. Back in the 1630s or somewhere around there, there was an outrageous demand for tulips. The Dutch went crazy for them. When the number of tulips began to multiply, the demand plummeted. Those who thought they had a valuable tulip had invested a huge sum. A few folks even risked their life savings, and they were left with nothing other than a worthless tulip."

"What prompted the tulip bubble?" Elisabeth asked.

"I am not completely sure, but maybe you could go online and find out. I never put much more thought into it. I just figured it was normal societal hysteria, the kind that comes and goes for no reason."

"I will have to remember to check that out," Elisabeth replied. "Well, you can have this beanie bear. Just make sure you never sell it, and please pass it down to your heirs."

"Ok, I will do exactly that," the attendant replied. She noticed that Elisabeth had a funny look on her face. Did she not understand something Elisabeth had told her? What had she missed?

"I promise to keep it for my own. I can't thank you enough, Elisabeth, it makes my whole day. It sure brings back some good memories of fun, carefree times. God bless you, dear."

Elisabeth said goodbye, signed the log for the visit, and walked out to her car.

Chapter 6 Jim

The sun was shining brightly, and Elisabeth could feel the warmth on her back. What a great day it was, and it just seemed to get better. She unlocked her car, and slipped into the driver's seat. She felt so at home. The car had warmed with the afternoon sun, and she felt a safe aura around her. She could only wonder if her grandma was looking down on her in that instant.

She put the key in the ignition, started the car, and rolled down the windows for some cool air. She took the beanie babies from her purse, and set them on the front seat.

Just as soon as she turned to look out the window, an incandescent white and blue butterfly floated in her window, and landed on a beanie baby. It stayed there for a minute, and waved its wings.

Elisabeth couldn't help but think about Grandma Ida, and she knew she was right there with her. Ida must have known Elisabeth was ready for the adventure. The butterfly leaped off the beanie, circled over the dashboard, and fluttered out her window.

Elisabeth could tell she was having one of those momentous lifetime feelings. She was at peace, and everything was right with the world. She knew her grandma would always be there for her. She took a deep breath, and thanked her grandma.

The car seemed to run better than she could ever remember, and she really needed to get going. Just then her phone rang, and jolted her back into the present. She opened her purse to find her phone. It wasn't a ringtone she had selected for anyone in particular, so she didn't know who was calling her. It was the default ringtone that was set up when she first got the phone.

"Hello, this is Elisabeth."

"Hey, this is Edward."

"Oh, I'm so glad it's you. How was your day?"

"It was fantastic! You won't believe it! Where are you?"

"I am downtown. I am just leaving the bank."

"Please come back to your grandma's house. I am here, and I have so much to tell you."

"I'll be right over."

A few minutes later, Elisabeth pulled into the familiar gravel driveway. She could see her grandma's car was already there. She walked up to the front porch, saw that the door was open, but knocked on the screen door anyway.

"Come on in," Edward said. "Wow, what a day. I couldn't wait to tell someone."

"Oh yeah, I had the craziest day too," Elisabeth said.

"I went down to English Lake, just like you told me," Edward said. "It was unbelievable. It's the majesty of two rivers joining together to flow as one. I was so amazed at how special it was, knowing all the history there. I could envision all the people that had come before, and enjoyed the same place. I wandered around and soaked up all the ambience I could. I saw this older guy fishing. He was the nicest guy. We talked a bit about where he was from, and I told him about how I had come here. He was so helpful and gave me some insight about a historical museum just east of English Lake in a town called Knox. He said they might be open, and since I was so close, I should at least drive over to check it out."

"Did you go then?" Elisabeth asked.

"Yes, I sure did. It was just a few minutes' drive, and let me tell you, driving around here is so nice. The roads are in great shape with wide lanes, and the people are generally nice drivers. It didn't take me long to get into town. It was really easy to find, just like the fisherman said. I pulled up to the old mansion, and it was a nice yellow house that sure showed its regal past. The porch was very inviting, so I parked right in front. I figured they probably would not be open, but I had to go look. When I went up to the front door, there was a sign that said they were only open on Friday, so I decided to just look around the porch and see all I could from there. I was walking down the porch steps to leave when the front door opened. When I turned to look, this tall, stately gentleman peered out."

"Can I help you?" he said.

"I nearly jumped out of my skin! It was so surreal. I spun around so quickly, and I really hope I didn't startle him. I said yes, he could help me. I told him where I was from, and why I was there. He was the nicest man anyone could meet. He said his name was Jim. He was the best. He invited me in, even though they were not officially open, and gave me the grand tour."

"The house was filled wall to wall with the most amazing history. I couldn't believe how much river history there was. The volumes of books on the table in the middle of the old, formal living room were astounding. I leafed through the books for a little bit, but I didn't want to take up all of his time. He was so nice to let me in on his day off. I was just looking around, and I found some old pictures of the English Lake area, and the hunters who used to go there. There were thousands of people who would hunt and fish. The pictures were almost not believable, but Jim assured me it was the same place I had just visited a few hours earlier. I could never imagine it was the same place. The pictures showed a vast expanse of flora and fauna. It was unreal. He said it was an everglade back in the day, one so huge it was impassable to most travelers. Only the hearty would make their way into the wetlands. He said it was the most important food source for the native Indians living there, and I can understand why. The whole area was a living, breathing ecosystem that provided a great bounty. The pictures of the river in those old books sure jumped out at me. Jim even showed me documents of old, local folklore. He had some tales of a bridge that was haunted by a dog headed lady! He said the tales never rang true, but the locals always liked to tell it anyway. A few brave ones go out to the old bridge, and return pretty scared. The old bridge is still there, but you have to walk to it now. I can't wait to go out there. If you want to come along, it sure would be fun. Then Jim had some information about a whole entire lake, with a large island in the middle that was home to a cast of wild bandits. He told me to go to the historical society in Newton County and ask about Bogus Island. That would be a great day trip, don't you think? Then he told me a story about a prince from wales who came here to hunt, but he left soon after because his trip was limited by unknown circumstances. He thought maybe the people at the Newton County Historical Society might know more about this, and maybe even the people from Illinois could help. He also suggested I try looking on that new-fangled, Internet thing. So that's why I rushed back here, to get on the computer to research. Oh, I am so sorry, I am being so rude. What was your great news?" Edward asked.

Elisabeth could only stare at him with an overloaded look. That was too much information for her brain to process, and she didn't even know where to begin. She wanted to hear more river tales, but her head felt like exploding.

"Oh, yeah? Well you have got to hear what I found out today!" she nearly shouted. "Oh my gosh, I went down to the bank today to take care of some accounts I have. I was checking on a safe deposit box I have there, when the attendant told me there was another one I was the curator of. I was so perplexed, but she insisted I was the person in charge of the box, so she brought it out and let me open it. Oh my gosh, I couldn't believe my eyes when I saw a letter in the box. Here, read this," Elisabeth said, and gave Edward the letter.

Chapter 7 Locket

"It is so amazing that my grandma would do something like this. I figured she took all her time up setting up the message in a bottle hunt, but apparently it's just a successor to this other treasure hunt with these beanie bear toys," Elisabeth said.

Edward read the letter and looked up at Elisabeth. "How in the world? How incredible is this? She was one wily woman, wasn't she?"

"Yes, who would have known? I mean one adventure is incredible, but two? Where did she find the time?" Elisabeth asked. "I have two of the beanies she left in the box and I am presuming she gave me this locket for a reason."

"Yes, it does have a unique shape," Edward said. "I never wanted to ask you because I didn't know if it was too personal, but I have never seen anyone wear a locket shaped that strangely. It is very unique. It's quirky and weird, but I thought since you were wearing it, you must really like it, and not think it is strange looking."

"I only wear it because Grandma gave it to me. At first, I didn't like wearing it much because it is so weird, but after she passed, I started wearing it more because it keeps me close to her," Elisabeth replied. "But now I know why she made sure I got it. She knew I would keep it safe. We need to get that trunk down here and see if it unlocks it. I am ready to explode with excitement!"

"Me too, let's get it down here," Edward said.

They both went up to the attic. The weight of the trunk was almost too much for them, but they worked hard, and managed to get it down the narrow staircase. Their adrenaline helped them get it into the parlor. They set it down and turned the front of it towards them.

"Well, here we go," Elisabeth said, as she unclasped the locket. She turned it to line up with the lock shape. She had to jiggle the locket into the opening, but it fit nicely and maybe just a little loose. Something snapped inside the latch and they both jumped back a bit. They looked at each other and laughed.

"Wow that freaked me out!" Elisabeth said.

"Me too," Edward said. "I thought the lock was going to pop open and something was going to spring out!"

Elisabeth laughed so hard she could hardly talk. "Yeah, me too. I was ready for anything when it comes to my grandma."

Elisabeth grabbed the locket and turned it a little. She heard another snap. That time they didn't move an inch. They were completely frozen. The latch stayed still for a moment, swung out, and hung from its hinge. They were both mesmerized.

"Do you want to do the honors?" Elisabeth asked.

"I think you are just scared. I will pull it open," Edward said, and reached for the top of the trunk. He grabbed the front corners and pulled strongly at them. They were tightly set in the matching bottom channel of the trunk. Edward put some more strength into it, and it finally gave way with the sound of sliding metal. The lid opened up easily at the hinge. The smell of antique leather and wood wafted out immediately from the trunk.

"Oh my," Elisabeth said.

"Look at all those," Edward said.

The lid was pushed open by the expanding stuffed figures inside, seeking their original size. The trunk was completely filled with beanie babies.

"Holy smokes! Look at all of them! I need to see the ones you got today. Go get them," he said.

Elisabeth ran and grabbed the ones she brought back from the bank. "Look, they all have the same blue ribbon on them," she said.

"Yes, they do," Edward said. "Let's get them out of there and line them up to compare."

Elisabeth agreed and they pulled them out, one by one, and lined them up on the parlor floor. They were all bears and no other sorts of animals.

"Hey, look at this!" Edward nearly yelled with excitement. "There is an envelope in here."

Edward pulled it out from the bottom, and it looked just like the one in the safe deposit box. "Your grandma was one amazing woman. Let's open it and see what she is up to now."

Edward opened the envelope and they both moved over to the sitting chairs.

"Hurry, what's in it?" Elisabeth asked.

Edward pulled out some sheets of paper. They were well typed, but the type set was not from a printer. "Looks like it was done on an old typewriter," he said.

"Yes, she did have a typewriter," Elisabeth said.

Edward was scanning the letter and Elisabeth started to get anxious. "Well, don't just read it to yourself, tell me what it says!"

"I'm sorry. I was just wrapped up in the moment. Let me go back to the start," he said, and began to read.

Welcome to another step in what should be a whole lot of fun. There are forty-seven beanie babies in this trunk. Each one can be uniquely identified in and of itself. The first identifier is the blue ribbon. In this envelope, you while find a piece of this blue ribbon to be able to verify its specific type, color, width, and texture. I have also left an end of one of the spools to further verify the exact ribbon I used so that you can be sure.

These forty-seven, along with the three I left in the safe deposit box, make up fifty of the two hundred I did. They are all uniquely identifiable and cannot be duplicated. The one hundred fifty remaining, that are not here, have been distributed throughout the United States, and some may have made it worldwide. The first marker is the ribbon on each of them, and it is the quickest way to see if someone has one that I did. There are other unique markers, and comparing these markers on each one will assure the owner they have one in their possession that is authentic. I have documented each of the ones I did in a list that spells out what type of beanie is one of the two hundred. The lists can be found with some clues I enclosed herein.

If you have the note from the safe deposit box, you will already know this is an adventure to be enjoyed and shared. There will be times this *may get out of control, but keep your foundation strong and stay true to yourself. This is an adventure for all to enjoy and please allow all who are good in heart to join in the fun. There will be those who try to derail the spirit of the good time, so take no actions against them, and pay them no heed. Their actions will not stand the test of time, and will wither on the vine as they are not true. Remember, keep everything in perspective and enjoy the adventure.*

Your friend watching over you, Ida

Elisabeth was stunned again and Edward was speechless. "This is nearly too much to comprehend," he finally said, but Elisabeth stayed silent.

"I came over here to track down the family heirloom, the coin, and now your grandma lays this on us. What do we do?" he asked.

Just then the phone rang and they nearly jumped out of their skin. They looked at each other in complete fright and were frozen in their chairs. Ring after ring, the old phone kept going. Elisabeth finally mustered up some strength to get up to answer the phone.

"Uh hello?" she said, in a quiet, frightened tone.

"Hello," the voice on the other end said. "Who is this?"

Chapter 8 Clues

Elisabeth's expression changed instantly and she let out a huge sigh of relief. "Oh Mom, this is Elisabeth."

"It didn't sound like you at all," Trinity replied on the other end. "I was calling to see if Edward was doing something for dinner. I just got back and was going to call him before I called you, but since you are there, you can ask him."

Elisabeth relayed this to Edward, who gave her an unsure look.

"Mom, could you go pick up some pizza and bring it over here? We would like to eat here and we need your help on some things," Elisabeth said. "Edward, my mom will be over in about thirty minutes. She wants to know what you want on your pizza."

Edward peered up from the papers he was looking over that were in the envelope. "No preference, get whatever you want," he said.

"No, Mom, he doesn't seem to mind, so just get our usual," Elisabeth said. "Thanks, Mom."

Elisabeth hung up and as soon as the handset hit the phone, they both burst out laughing hysterically. After a few minutes, they looked at each other and caught their breath.

"Whew," Elisabeth said. "I thought for sure that was going to be a haunted moment."

"Yeah, me too," Edward said. "I wasn't going to pick up that phone. I thought it would be your grandma on the other end channeling through it."

"I was petrified, but I had to answer it just in case it was!" she laughed.

"Maybe it really was your grandma speaking through your mom."

"Oh, you could be right. Maybe that's how I found the courage to answer. My mom should be by in half an hour with pizza for us."

"Good, then maybe she can help us with this wild adventure. She seems very steady when it comes to these things, but maybe because it was her mom and she knew her best," Edward said.

"Let's count the beanie babies to make sure there are forty-seven here, and then get the table ready for dinner," Elisabeth said.

With the windows open to let the evening breeze in, the curtains flowed gracefully back and forth, like a whimsical play of nature. The sound of a car pulling up outside drifted in through the open windows.

"Mom's here," Elisabeth said. "Quick, we need to get the table ready."

Elisabeth ran into the kitchen and pulled out the plates and cups from the cabinet. Edward grabbed the napkins and enough silverware to make three place settings.

"You guys here?" Trinity called out as she entered the front door.

"Yes, Mom, we're in the kitchen."

Trinity brought the pizzas in and set them down in the middle of the table. "The table looks nice," she said. "Get your piece. I am so hungry."

"Yes, thanks for coming. I would have forgotten to eat if you hadn't called," Elisabeth said.

"That's not possible, Elisabeth, you are the last person to forget to eat, unless it's something really important. So what is so important?" Trinity asked, as she grabbed a slice of pizza and took a bite.

"I went to the bank today, and was checking on my accounts when the attendant told me I had another safe deposit box. After I finally agreed to look in it, I found a letter that told me to look in the attic for a trunk, and to use my locket for the key. So Edward and I went up to the attic and brought the trunk down here to open. We put it in the parlor," Elisabeth said.

"Really? I have got to see this," Trinity said, and got up with the pizza in her hand and went into the parlor. "What in the world is all this?" she exclaimed. "Where did you two get all these toys? What is going on? Is this some sort of joke you're playing on me?"

"No, it's not a joke. This is the trunk we opened with my locket. All of these toys were in there. I also have three more that were in the safe deposit box. There are fifty of them all together. This is all Grandma's doing!" Elisabeth said.

"Your grandma did this?" Trinity asked. "Oh, this is going to be good. She was one wily woman wasn't she? Why did she put these toys in the trunk? This ought to be fun."

"We found a note along with them," Edward said. He handed Trinity the note. "It has a lot of detail, but it sure leaves a lot out too."

"Yeah, Mom, this is really crazy and we are not sure what to do. We are glad you called because we need your advice on this one," Elisabeth said.

Trinity put the note down on the end table and looked over at Elisabeth with a truly stunned look. "Oh my, oh my, we need to think about this. This is out of control. We need to really think about this."

"That's why we need your help. We are in way over our heads here," Edward said.

"If this is what I think it is, we need to
strategize and make a plan. First, let's outline what
we know. We know we have fifty beanie bears
and there are one hundred fifty others out there.
Each one is unique, and can be verified as
authentic. We are not sure about how to verify
each one's authenticity, but we know there is a list
of the type of beanie that was used. We have some
clues as to what's on the list, but we don't have
the list. Now, let's think about how this might play
out. If we can find the list of the types that she
made, and if we don't know how to authenticate
them, then all we have are these fifty to look at,
because we know these are verified to be the ones
she made. We know she used a specific blue
ribbon on each of them, and we have the evidence
to prove the blue ribbon. So first of all, we need to
secure the blue ribbon and its unique qualities in
the safe deposit box, so we can be well assured the
three of us are the only living people who know
the type of blue ribbon. Now people will know
right away the original two hundred have blue
ribbons on them, but they will not be sure of the
type of blue ribbon. So tomorrow, Elisabeth, take
the blue ribbon spool, and the note, and put them

into the safe deposit box where you found the beanies," Trinity said.

"Ok Mom," Elisabeth said.

"Now we have these fifty we know are authentic," Trinity said, as she pointed to the ones lined up on the floor.

"Well Mom," Elisabeth quietly chimed in.

"What? What is it?"

"I gave one to the attendant at the bank, but I didn't tell her anything about the unique quality."

"Well, that's alright, I guess. The note said to share the adventure and you did just that. This will be good because she will be assured she has an authentic one," Trinity said. "So then, let's look at the ones we have, and write down what we know." Trinity picked up one from the floor and told Edward to take notes.

"I'm ready," Edward said.

"Let's see," Trinity said.

Elisabeth picked another one up and began to look at it from all sides. "The ribbon seems to match the description on the note," she said.

"Yes it does," Trinity replied.

"I see they have these plastic protectors on every one of the tags," Edward said.

"Those were put on when they were new. Back when these were highly collectable, it was a big thing to have a protector on each tag. It maintained the collectability, and kept the tag from getting messed up," Trinity explained.

"But each of these have the same round, heavy plastic tag on them," Elisabeth said.

"They had different kinds of tags back in those days. There were thin, plastic ones and there were also more expensive, thicker ones with rounded edges. The thicker ones came out first. The thinner ones came out later when the collectability really took off. Knowing your grandma, she would have used the better ones, so we know all of these have the same thick plastic covers," Trinity said.

"That's one clue," Edward said. "I'm writing it down."

"What else can we see about these?" Trinity asked.

Elisabeth was holding one and turned it around in her hands.

"Ow!" she said all of a sudden. "What was that?"

"What is wrong?" Trinity asked.

"I don't know, but I just got poked on my finger by something!"

Elisabeth moved the beanie bear around and tried to feel where there might have been something sharp on it. "Oh there it is. I see it," she said.

"See what? What is it?" Edward said excitedly.

"I'm not sure, but it's pretty sharp, and it's in the seam of the right ear, where the ear is sewn onto the head," she said.

Edward turned the one he was holding to get a better look at it. He turned it to the right side, and stretched out the ear. "I have one too," he said.

"Yeah, I have one too, on this one," Trinity said.

"It looks like a staple," Edward said.

"I think so too," Elisabeth said. "It's a staple, a common staple. Well, there is our second clue, a staple in the seam on the right ear. Let's check the others to see if they have it too."

They picked up each one. Sure enough, each one of them had the same staple in the seam of the right ear.

"So, she stapled each one of them in the exact same place. Alright, let's keep our heads together, and keep looking for more clues," Trinity said.

They kept looking at the beanies to see what else they could discover about them. It took them well into the night, but they couldn't seem to find any more similarities.

"I need to go home and get some sleep," Trinity said. "You too, Elisabeth."

"Yes, Mom. Goodnight, Edward. See you in the morning," Elisabeth said.

"I am already looking forward to it," Edward said.

Chapter 9 Code

The morning broke and Trinity and Elisabeth showed up early, only to find Edward already up and making breakfast.

"Come on in!" Edward said.

They went in and saw that the parlor was just like they left it last night. Edward was making breakfast and it smelled so good it made Elisabeth's stomach growl.

"Boy, that smells good," Elisabeth said.

"I made enough for all of us if you are hungry," Edward replied.

"Oh, yes, I am hungry," Elisabeth said.

"Me, too," Trinity agreed.

They ate at the kitchen table and went over the last night's clues.

"Edward, I thought you would stay up all night checking the beanies out to see if you could find anything else," Elisabeth said. "I would have if I were you," she quipped.

"I thought about it, but I was so tired. I went right to sleep. It's so easy to sleep well here," Edward said.

"Yeah, I know," Trinity said. "It always was a peaceful place to sleep."

They finished their breakfast and returned to the parlor to look at the beanie bears.

"I will look on the Internet to see if there are any clues to help us," Elisabeth said.

"Yeah, that might help," Edward said.

Trinity was scanning each of the toys, but couldn't find any new differences in them.

"Wait," Edward said. "I see this tag has red on the outer edge. I can see it inside the tag protector. It goes all the way around the outer edge of the tag. Did they all get made like that?"

"I don't know, but I could look it up," Elisabeth said.

"Each one of these has a red mark on the outer edge of the tag!" Trinity said. "I see it right here. The tags didn't have a red outline on them when they were made, so it must be something Grandma did to each one. So we have three clues to authenticate each of these, but we don't know where the list is that describes the type of all of them she did."

Edward looked at the note again. "What about this note that was in the trunk? On the bottom it says LPHA 3a1598, LPCRO 98a12315."

"It looks like some kind of code," Trinity said.

"It does, but I wonder what it means?" Elisabeth said. "We need to read both of the notes again to see if there are clues."

They reread both notes several times, but it seemed the cryptic writing at the bottom had no correlation to the other note from the safe deposit box.

"Hmm, maybe we should look around the house to see if there is something here that reveals a clue to the code," Elisabeth said.

"I will check the bedroom and the living room," Edward said.

NCPL
Morocco Community Library
205 S. West Street
P O Box 87
Morocco, IN 47963

"I'll check the kitchen," Trinity said. "Elisabeth, you look in the parlor and the foyer."

They searched high and low, but nothing seemed to relate to the letters and numbers. The pictures on the wall were all floral landscapes with blue backgrounds, and the knick knacks were typical for a house of its age. Elisabeth checked the bureau and sifted through the papers inside, but nothing out of the ordinary stood out.

"Well, I have nothing," Edward said.

"Neither do we," Elisabeth and Trinity replied.

"Edward, grab those post-it notes over there. We will write down the letters and numbers so we can each have a reference if we run into anything or get an idea of what they mean. Then Elisabeth will take the note and the beanies to the bank tomorrow to put them in safe deposit boxes," Trinity said.

"That sounds like a good plan to me," Edward said.

"I can do that," Elisabeth replied.

They each wrote down the letters and numbers on a post-it note and put it in their pocket. Elisabeth and Edward got the beanies and the notes, and put them in a bag for the trip to the bank.

Trinity looked at Edward and Elisabeth. "Alright, we are set now. This needs to stay with each of us until we have a sensible plan to tackle this adventure Grandma has set up. It may, and probably will, get very tense, but we need to stick together and keep it fun."

"I am good with that," Edward said.

"Me too," Elisabeth agreed.

"Well, I need to get going because I have to get up for work. Let's keep thinking about the notes and get back together later tomorrow," Trinity said.

Trinity and Elisabeth quickly helped Edward tidy up the parlor before they made their way out to their cars in the driveway. Edward saw them to the front door and closed it behind them. He was thinking that this was a lot of fun and staying there was so nice. He couldn't wait to get some more of the truly restful sleep. He wondered how he would get back to tracking down the coin he came here for. The night was pleasant and passed by in an instant.

The next morning, the sun shone in between the curtains, and woke Edward up from his sound sleep. He was so well rested, he had no problem getting up, and he went to get something to eat. As he was sitting at the kitchen table, eating the eggs and bacon he made, he glanced over to the things he set down on the end table near the foyer.

"Oh, yeah," he thought to himself. "Those are the brochures I brought back from Starke County." He lifted up the top one. It was a pamphlet from the Newton County Museum.

"Oh, it looks like they are open today. I need to go down there to see if I can find something that will guide me to the coin," he thought, and just then the phone rang.

"Hello, it's Elisabeth," he heard on the other end.

"Oh hey, I was just looking at some of the stuff I brought back yesterday. I found a brochure for the Newtown County Historical Museum. I was thinking about going down there today. What do you think?" he asked.

"Well, it's a good drive, and I am free if you don't mind me tagging along," Elisabeth said. "I can be there in about 45 minutes."

"That would be fun," he said. "Come on over and I will be ready."

Chapter 10 Newton

Elisabeth pulled up on time, just like she said. Edward saw her, grabbed his car keys and backpack, and locked the front door.

"Do you want me to drive?" he asked, as he walked down the sidewalk.

"Sure, that would be a good idea. Grandma's car probably needs some highway time anyway," Elisabeth said.

"Then hop in and we will get going."

They climbed into Ida's car and made their way out toward the west side of town.

"I need to stop and get some gas. Is that ok, or should we wait until we get there?" Edward asked.

"No, it's probably best to get gas here. It will most likely be cheaper here in town."

Edward pulled into the gas station to fill up and Elisabeth decided to get some snacks for the drive.

"Good idea," Edward said. "Will you grab me a chocolate frosted donut and some chocolate milk?"

"Yes, I will. You will need the energy because it will take about an hour to drive there. There is no good way to get there from here. The old state roads are nice and all, but if you get stuck behind slow cars or tractors with farm equipment, it could take forever," Elisabeth said with a smile.

"Good thing I'm not in a hurry. Go get our food and off we will go!" Edward quipped.

They cruised down the two lane state roads, and the scenery was typical country farmsteads. They looked magnificent in the early morning sunlight, so peaceful and serene. Edward seemed to be so at ease with driving, even though they occasionally got behind some slow moving vehicles. He took it all in stride, and seemed to be at one with the traffic, and they made their way to the museum.

"I have to say," Edward said, breaking the silence that filled the car, except for the radio quietly playing in the background. "The roads over here are so comfortable to drive on and the people seem, for the most part, easy to drive with. I mean, some are inconsiderate and arrogant, but most are very polite. They actually stay in their lane and signal their intents. I am just not used to that."

"Well, I never thought of it before, but you are right. The people do seem to be generally helpful, especially when you drive these state roads out in the rural areas," Elisabeth replied. "Maybe the scenery has a calming effect and they realize life doesn't always have to be so tense," she continued.

"Whoa, wait, do we turn off here?" he exclaimed.

"Oh, yeah, turn here. Turn here and go south."

Edward turned and got on the interstate. The car easily accelerated into the on-ramp and got up to speed. It seemed to enjoy the chance to show its prowess on the interstate once again. The engine spun like a well-timed pocket watch, or a finely tuned sewing machine just spinning along, as happy as could be.

"Hey there, Tex," Elisabeth said. "You need to watch the speed limit."

"Oh, yeah," Edward said. "I was so enjoying the car singing along I let it get away from me." He slowed the car down, but still stayed a few miles per hour over the speed limit.

"That's better. We are not in any break neck hurry."

"These lanes on the interstate are the best," he said. "They are so wide, and the shoulders are almost as wide. I could drive all day and night and not run off the road. See, the pavement is everywhere out here," and he edged across the fog line. The car started to rumble very loudly.

"What the heck?" he shouted and straightened the car back into the lane. "What the heck was that? I thought the car was going to rattle apart. Did I break something?" Edward was visibly trembling. He had a death grip on the steering wheel with both hands.

"You sure didn't see that coming did you? They call those rumble strips," Elisabeth laughed.

84

"Rumble what?"

"Rumble strips. They put them on the edges of the road to alert drivers who may doze off. The noise and the vibration alert them to get back into the driving lane."

"Rumble strips? More like heart attack makers! That scared me to death! I thought the car was about to completely break into pieces."

"That's the point."

"Then why in the heck do they make the shoulders so wide then?" Edward asked.

"My dad tells me they make them wide because people don't want to take responsibility for their own actions. When they aren't paying attention, they get into an accident. He said the wide shoulders and clear zones are to make sure the driver has a chance to correct themselves before they get into big trouble. That way, if they do get in an accident, they will have less to sue for, but they still won't want to admit they were the ones who were being irresponsible in their driving."

"I guess I can see that," Edward said.

"When we drive, we are required to drive without distractions. No talking on the phone, no eating, and no putting on makeup. We are to concentrate, because the driver is responsible for their vehicle, the people in it, and the people sharing the road with them. Around here, people always try to blame others for their lack of attention, and they never want to admit responsibility," Elisabeth preached.

"Your dad is right. If everyone obeyed those rules, it would make for an easier drive on these interstates. Oh, is this our exit?"

"Yes, turn off here. This way will get us over to Kentland."

They slowly turned off the interstate, and were back on a state road.

"This is so much of a calmer drive," Edward said.

"Yes, it is nice," Elisabeth agreed.

They traveled for a while to another divided state road before turning south at the sign directing them to Kentland.

"It's not too far from here," Elisabeth said. "Just a few miles down this highway."

They traveled south a little ways farther. As he was driving, Edward could see the vast expanse of farm ground and one large hill over to the right.

"Is that large hill the one I heard about when I was in Starke County? Is that what they call Bogus Island?"

"I am not sure. It could be. My grandma once told me a little bit of history about Beaver Lake and Bogus Island. It would make sense, because it's the only large hill out here. The rest of this flat ground could have been the lake bed."

"That would make sense," Edward said.

"It looks like there is a road coming up on the right, just at the bottom of the hill. Turn in there so we can check it out," Elisabeth said.

"Will do!" Edward replied, and he entered the deceleration lane. He turned off the highway and onto an old looking bridge. He looked closer and realized it was really a new bridge, and that it was just made to look old by using wood for the deck and the side rails.

"Look there at that sign. It says this is the ditch that drained Beaver Lake," Edward said.

"Oh wow, pull over there and park. I want to get some pictures of it," Elisabeth said.

They pulled the car over into a small, graveled area. Edward noticed a plaque next to it that memorialized the site. As they got out, they could hear the sound of a babbling brook. It was the ditch they had just passed over and it was extremely deep. It had steep sides, and did not appear to be natural.

"Well, look at that," Edward said. "The ditch was dug right through here to let the water past this high area. It drained the lake, according to that plaque over there."

"That is kind of sad."

"Yes, it is kind of sad, but look at all the farm ground it created." He pointed to the vast openness of the planted fields.

"Well, you are right. That is a lot of food."

"But this can't be the Bogus Island I was told of. This must have been the north side of the lake, because the water in the ditch is flowing north towards the Kankakee River. We passed over that a while ago."

"You might be right. The island should be a little south of here. Let's get back on the highway to see if we can discern where it was. It should be a large hill not too far from here," Elisabeth said.

"Let's go," Edward agreed and started toward the car.

In no time, they were back onto the highway and up to speed.

"I don't see anything out here," Elisabeth said.

"Me neither," Edward replied. "Wait, look at that!"

It came out of nowhere, a large billboard that read "The Former Site of Bogus Island."

"So there is our answer," Elisabeth said. "It's all gone! There is nothing left! Oh, that is truly sad."

"It must have been magnificent in its day, despite its checkered past."

They continued to drive past the billboard, the buildings next to it, and on across the wide, open, flat farmland. After a couple of long curves, they could see some large grain elevators up ahead.

"I see grain towers, so I presume we are getting closer to Kentland?" Elisabeth asked.

"I would presume so."

When they came up to the highway stop light, they saw a sign that pointed them toward the downtown area.

"Here we are then," Edward said. "The downtown is to the right. I think the museum is just a couple of blocks down this road."

"Oh, it's right there, so park in that lot next to it."

As Edward parked, Elisabeth saw several people inside. They were all sitting in a small circle. The building looked like an old grocery store, before grocery stores became mega sized.

Edward and Elisabeth entered the glass doors and went inside. The people sitting in the circle suddenly stopped talking, and turned to see who had just come in.

Chapter 11 History

The room was filled with the pungent scent of historical inventory. The walls were covered floor to ceiling with bookshelves housing books and maps from all ages. One map in particular was front and center, and showed a big area of water drawn on it. There was a large island in the middle labeled Bogus Island. The lake was named Beaver Lake. Edward was mesmerized.

The lady sitting the farthest away turned and faced them.

"Hello, how are you doing today?" she asked.

"Very well, thank you. We are from LaPorte County and we came to check out some history of the Kankakee," Elisabeth said.

"Well you came to the right place! We are steeped in Kankakee history. There is so much to show. Where do you want to start?" the curator asked.

"How about that map," Edward chimed in.

"Oh, that map? Yes, that map shows what the area was like before it got drained."

"We just drove past that. We saw a ditch with a sign that said it drained the lake," Edward said.

"That is true. That is the ditch that drained the lake. We had the sign put up to tell people some of our local history. It's not the nicest part of our history, but it is what it is."

"We can see where the lake bed is, but the island is gone. What ever happened to the island? How can you move a whole island? It was big, wasn't it?" Edward asked.

"Yes, it was quite large," the curator replied. "But I presume you came here on Highway 41?"

"Yes, we were driving from the north, and heading south on a divided highway," Edward said.

"You were on a divided highway, but if you look on this map, Highway 41 was an old state highway with only two lanes. It was the major road from Chicago to Indianapolis. But it got so congested they needed to add travel lanes, so voila, there you have it, a divided highway. It's safer and can handle more traffic," the curator explained.

"But what does that have to do with Bogus Island?" Elisabeth asked. "I see on the map the old state road didn't go through the island."

"Oh, you are quick!" the curator said. "You see, the land surrounding the island was the old lake bed. It was drained by the farmers so they could farm the rich ground with higher yielding crops. But it was still low ground, and prone to flooding, so there was no way the engineers would build more roads and leave it open to possible flooding. That would create an immense traffic hazard."

"Yeah, Elisabeth's dad is an engineer. He has told her all about the liability of not having safe driving lanes. If they were to build a new roadway, and something happened to someone because of water on the road, surely it would not be good," Edward said.

"Yes, my dad, the engineer, would have made sure the new road was high enough so that it would not flood, and that there was a place for the water to drain off the pavement," Elisabeth said.

"Sounds like you have it all figured out," the curator responded.

"Huh," Edward sighed. "The road had to be high enough to be safe, but where do you think they got enough material to build the road on?"

Elisabeth and Edward's faces both lit up and they realized at the same moment what happened with the road.

"Bogus Island!" they both exclaimed in unison.

The curator smiled and said, "See now, you are already learning about the history of our area."

"That is so cool," Edward said. "The island was put under the new roadway!"

"I guess we sort of drove over the island," Elisabeth said.

"Yes, I guess you did, sadly enough," the curator said.

They spent the rest of the day looking at everything the time allowed them. They couldn't get to everything in the museum, but with the help of the curator, they saw all they needed to see for one day. They were able to learn a lot about how it all related to the Kankakee River and its historic past.

The day ran long, and the curator could tell she had overloaded them with knowledge.

"You've given us a lot of information," Elisabeth said. "I am so well informed I don't know where to start."

"Me too," Edward said. "But I have one question about something. I know the Prince of Wales came here to visit and hunt, but then he left quickly. I don't see any record of him hunting here."

"Well, that could be because he was not here diplomatically, he was just here on a recreational visit to hunt, so no formal record was kept," the curator said.

"I was doing some research online about the prince, and the details are sketchy at best. I did find that after he was here, he was sent to Persia and Mesopotamia. His mother, the queen, sent him there on a trip. The history records only vaguely reference his trip here and his trip to the Far East," Edward said.

"So, what are you saying?" the curator asked.

"All I am saying is that it seems strange a prince would come here to hunt, but leave quickly on a trip to the Far East. Would it make sense that there was something he was looking for?" Edward asked.

"I never thought of it that way," the curator said. "What do you think he was doing?"

"I am not sure, but I will keep looking and researching until I find out," Edward said.

"That sounds like it will be fun. All I ask is that if you find out more information about the prince and his travels to the Kankakee Marsh, would you let us know?" the curator asked.

"Absolutely, I will do that," Edward said.

It was getting late and Elisabeth was feeling completely worn out. Just as they were leaving, Elisabeth decided to thank the other curator for all her help, so she went over to shake her hand. As soon as she got to the main desk where the curator was sitting, Elisabeth saw it.

Elisabeth turned to Edward and knew he saw it too. "Oh, wow," she thought, and she knew Edward was thinking the same. They couldn't believe it. It couldn't be. There was no way.

Elisabeth tried to stay calm as she offered her hand to the curator.

"That is a nice beanie baby you have there," Elisabeth said.

"Oh, that old thing? It's been sitting there for so long. I need to dust it," the curator said.

"It is so pretty," Elisabeth said. "I really like the blue ribbon on it."

Edward coughed loudly and Elisabeth turned to him. He was cringing and smirking at her. She gave him the 'I know and I will keep quiet' look and then mouthed 'it's ok'.

"Yes, the ribbon was on it when I found it at my church bazaar jamboree. I just had to have it for some reason," the curator said.

"I think it's so cute. You should definitely dust it off and take good care of it. You never know when they will come back into vogue," Elisabeth said, as she smiled.

Edward grabbed Elisabeth's arm tightly and abruptly escorted her out the door. The curators looked puzzled, but just shrugged their shoulders.

"How strange was that? Well, whatever, let's lock up and go home," the curator said.

Edward kept quiet until they were safely in the car and out of earshot.

"What are you doing?" Edward demanded. "I was sure you were going to say something! We don't even know what we have yet!"

"I know! I was dying to say something, but I just wanted her to know how important it was for her to keep it safe, just in case this turns out to be true," Elisabeth said.

"That beanie has lasted this long just sitting there, so it should still be there later on."

"That's what I thought, so I left it alone," Elisabeth said.

"Good, because we are not ready yet. Your mom needs to get a plan together for how we are to get this out there, but only after we verify all of it," Edward said.

"Well, that just started the verification process, didn't it?" Elisabeth said.

"Yes, I guess you are right, it sure did. Your grandma must have been down here."

"Yes, that proves she was here. Let's get going, I want to get home at a decent hour."

The drive home was pleasant and the traffic was light. They decided to take the interstate home instead of the back roads. It was a few miles longer, but it took less time.

The quietness inside the car was not uncomfortable. Elisabeth knew that Edward was deep in thought processing the information he learned from the trip to the museum, along with everything else he had researched on the Internet.

She was happy to let the silence fill the cabin, and relished the solace. The car ran beautifully, and the finely tuned engine purred all the way back. Elisabeth had nearly dozed off when she woke to the sound of the gravel driveway at her grandma's house.

"Wake up, Elisabeth. We are home," Edward said.

Elisabeth poured herself out of the car and thanked Edward for the wonderful day.

"I will see you later, Edward," she said.

"Yeah, see you later. I will call you," Edward said.

Chapter 12 Downtown

It was later in the afternoon the next day, when Elisabeth walked in the front door of her home. The house smelled of a well cooked dinner and the normal, serene atmosphere was welcoming.

"Is that you, Elisabeth?" Trinity called.

"Yes, it's me, Mom. I am just getting back from class."

"Oh, good, dinner is almost ready. It's just you and I tonight. Your father is working late, or was he going to a meeting? I don't remember."

Elisabeth set her books down in the den before going into the half bath to wash her hands for dinner.

"Ok, I am ready to eat," Elisabeth said, as she went into the kitchen.

"Grab a napkin and some silverware for both of us and we can start eating," Trinity said.

They devoured dinner in no time and almost forgot to leave some for Elisabeth's dad.

103

"I think we need to talk, don't we, Elisabeth?"

"Yes, we do. I haven't had time to tell you about the trip to the museum and what we saw when we were there. The curator had a blue ribbon beanie bear on her desk! Edward and I both saw it ourselves."

"Did you say anything to her?"

"No, I didn't. Edward nearly dragged me out of there so I wouldn't. But I did tell her to keep it safe, because you never know when it could be worth something again."

"Well, that was probably best. So do you think it was one of them?"

"I am pretty sure. The lady said she got it from her church bazaar jamboree, so you never know. Maybe Grandma planted it there. Maybe she planted others too. Who knows how many could be down there?"

"Yes, this is getting fun, but we have to first do some homework on the authenticity of this whole scheme she made up. We don't want to go out half right about the whole thing and start mass hysteria, just in case it turns out to be a wild goose chase," Trinity said.

"I am a little scared of the whole thing. If it's just a made up adventure, and it gets out of control, and then we find out it's not real, or it can't be verified, then people will come after us," Elisabeth said.

"That would be very bad. We need to be very careful here, but just to find that a beanie is actually out there is amazing," Trinity said. "I think I have a plan. Tomorrow, I need to go turn in the tax payment for Grandma's house. Then we can get together with Edward, and review what we know."

"That sounds good to me. I am free tomorrow."

The next day was a beautiful day, and Trinity was up and ready to go. Elisabeth drug herself downstairs and tried to find something to eat.

"Are you in a hurry, Mom?"

"No, I'm just looking over the tax bills to make sure we get them right before I go down there. You know what a pain it is making sure I am paying the correct amount out of the right account. If I mess it up, I will have to document it at the end of the year with the accountant and that is no fun, to say the least."

Elisabeth ate a bowl of cereal and went into the den to get her phone off the charger. The den was filled with a special aura. As soon as she entered, she sensed the academic overtone. It had always put her into the right mindset, since she first started early grade school until now in her college career.

She went to the table with the octopus of cords and chargers on it. Her phone was the one sitting on top of the black tablet. When she picked it up, she accidentally hit the power button on the side. The screen flashed that the battery was fully charged, and it booted up to show she had a message.

"Hmm," she said. "Who could that be?"

She swiped the recent calls screen and saw it was from Edward. She was sure he wanted to talk about the museum trip.

"Mom, Edward called and left a message, so I will call him on our way out. Are you ready?"

"Yes, just let me get my purse."

Trinity followed Elisabeth through the kitchen and into the garage.

"Are you ready now? Do you have everything you need?" Trinity asked.

"Who, me? You are the one who needs to make sure you have everything you need to pay that tax bill," Elisabeth said, and smiled.

"Don't give me that look. Soon you will be paying tax bills for your own home."

"I know, but now it's fun to hassle you!" Elisabeth said, and smirked wildly at her mom.

They drove toward the center of town where the courthouse was. Elisabeth swiped her phone out of sleep mode, and pushed the recent calls list to return the call to Edward.

"Hello?" he said.

"Edward, this is Elisabeth. I saw you called."

"Did you listen to the message I left?"

"No, I just called you back. What's up?"

"We need to go over this whole adventure thing."

"I am with my mom right now," Elisabeth said. "We could come over to pick you up. We are on our way to the courthouse. My mom has to pay a property tax bill. Do you want to tag along?"

"Oh, that would be fun. Come and get me, then I can scout around to see what I can find there."

"Ok, see you in a few minutes. Bye, bye."

Edward was ready and waiting on the porch when they pulled up. He got in the back seat and made himself comfortable. It only took Trinity a few minutes to drive to the main street in town, where she slowed down so Edward could get a good look at the old storefronts.

He saw a very large, old, castle looking building that was surrounded by a knee high stone wall. He could tell right away it had been the center of town for the longest time.

"Is that the courthouse?" Edward asked.

"Yes, that is the old courthouse, but we need to go into that other building to pay the tax bills," Trinity said.

"Can I go in the old courthouse?" he begged.

"Well, yeah, I am sure we can, but after we pay the bills," Trinity said.

"Then I am in!" he said, excitedly.

They found a parking space across the street and made their way to the entrance. They walked over a brick paved sidewalk to a quirky door at the corner of the building. It faced the street at an angle, and almost opened into the column on the very corner of the building.

"Let me help you with the door," Edward said, as he saw a guy coming out. The man had his

109

hands full carrying a suitcase type of box and some strange looking pole.

"Thank you, Sir. We were just heading out. Have a good day, Sir," the man said, as he hurried by.

Edward held the door open for everyone, and they all wandered in.

Chapter 13 Offices

The foyer of the building had some computer terminals along the opposite wall. There were a couple of people standing in the middle of the hallway looking around like they were lost and had no way to find out where to go.

"Where do we go, Mom?" Elisabeth asked.

"Well, I am not sure. Maybe we should just go in here. They might be able to help us."

Edward grabbed the door handle of the only visible door there, and pulled, but it didn't open.

"I think you should push," Elisabeth said.

"Oh, I see," he said. He pushed the door open and held it for them to go in. The counter was tall and long. It had some map books piled up on one end, and a large, leafy plant on the other end that was seemingly out of place.

"That is weird," Edward said. "Typically, the door should open out for fire safety. If you were in this room, and had to get out fast, you would push the door to go out. But if you were

111

flustered, you would waste precious seconds pushing on that door. The people behind you would be pushing on you too, and you might not be able to pull the door open to get out."

"That makes sense," Trinity said. "I never think about things like that."

"Can we help you?" a voice behind the desk asked.

"Oh, yes, we are here to pay this tax bill and we aren't sure where to go," Trinity said.

A nice lady came up to the counter, and helped them get to where they needed to go.

"Just go down the hall and to the left, the Treasurer's Office," she pointed.

"Thanks a lot. Sorry to bother you," Trinity said.

"Oh, it's no problem," the lady replied.

They went back out, and down the hallway to the office to pay the taxes. While they were walking toward the other office, Elisabeth got the strangest look on her face, and stopped cold in her tracks.

"What's wrong, Elisabeth?" Edward asked quietly.

Trinity was already out of sight, on her way to take care of her business. Elisabeth looked at Edward and pointed to the information board on the wall.

"Edward! Edward!" she said excitedly. "Look there on that board."

"Yeah, so what about it?"

"Don't you see it there? Right there!" and she put her finger right on the glass.

"Are you kidding me?" he said a bit too loudly. "This cannot be. There is no way this could be." He reached into his pocket, and pulled the post-it note from his wallet. He took a good look at it. "We need to go get your mom right now."

They both walked deliberately fast down the hallway and turned quickly into the office. Trinity was at the counter, in front of the glass partition, taking her receipt, when Elisabeth hurried up next to her. She grabbed her arm tightly.

"Mom!" she said. "You have got to see this."

"Hold on, hold on. Let me put this receipt away," Trinity said annoyingly.

The employee behind the glass gave them a strange, bothersome look.

"What is it?" Trinity said.

"It's out here, down here in the hall," Edwards said. "You have got to see this."

They led Trinity back down the hall and near the entrance door. They pointed to the information board that listed all of the offices in the building. One of them was the Recorder's Office.

"Is it possible?" Elisabeth asked.

"Let's see," Trinity replied, and she pulled out her post-it note from her coin purse. Her face lit up like Christmas morning and she was stunned solid.

"Well, there is only one way to tell. We just need to go to that office and ask them for this number, right?" Edward asked.

"It would seem so," Trinity said. "But be calm about it. No matter what happens, or what we are shown, do not say anything! Just keep calm until we get back to the car."

"Ok," Edward and Elisabeth nodded their heads in agreement.

They found the stairs to be very steep, but they had good traction all the way to the second floor. Right at the top of the stairs, they saw the plaque for the office and went in.

"Not this time," Edward thought. "I am going to push this door to open it. I learned my lesson on the last door." He pushed the door open, and smiled with satisfaction.

The office had another tall counter, but it was longer, and had less stuff on it. The employees were all working behind their

115

monitors, and seemed quite diligent in their work. The clerk to the left of the very end looked up and smiled.

"How can I help you?" she asked.

"Well, we aren't sure, but we are looking for something. We have this," Trinity said, and she wrote down a number on a scrap piece of paper and handed it to the nice lady.

"It looks like you need a deed record. I can get that for you. There is a charge of one dollar though."

"That's ok," Trinity replied.

Edward and Elisabeth were standing at Trinity's side in a completely frozen, statuesque way. They looked like they had just seen a spirit, and didn't seem to be moving, let alone barely breathing.

"Here it is, right here," the lady said. "It looks like a recorded survey. Does that seem like what you are looking for?"

"Um, well," Trinity stuttered. She was also frozen, and could barely find the strength or will

116

to answer. "I am not sure. You said it's a survey? A survey of what?"

"It looks like a survey of a house. I will print it out for you to get a better look. If it's not what you want, I will not charge you," the lady said.

The employee pressed some buttons, and got up to go over to the printer. The printer spooled up quickly, and the copy swiftly came out of the top. She grabbed it seamlessly as soon as it came out, and in one well practiced motion, she placed it on the counter in front of them.

"Is this what you are looking for?" she asked.

Trinity looked at it for only a brief second and was completely speechless. She absolutely couldn't find the will to speak. She could only stare at the print. Edward and Elisabeth were also stuck in time, and had nearly stopped breathing.

"Are you alright?" the lady asked.

"Yes," Trinity managed to get out quietly, but she still didn't move.

"Is this what you need?" the lady asked again.

"Yes," Trinity managed.

"That will be one dollar, please," the lady said.

In an instinctive reaction, Trinity reached into her purse. She got out a one dollar bill, and put it on the counter. Her eyes had not budged from the paper.

"Do you need a receipt?" the lady asked.

Edward chimed in now because he could see Elisabeth and Trinity were completely stunned. "No, we don't. This will be fine. Thank you very, very much," he said. He picked up the paper, and turned toward the door.

Elisabeth and Trinity, as if under some magical spell, hypnotically followed Edward, who was carrying the paper, out the door. Edward turned the opposite direction of the stairs, and led them into a more secluded place before turning to them.

"This is unbelievable," he said.

118

"Yes, I thought I was going to faint," Trinity said.

"I was not prepared for her to give us a print of my grandma's house," Elisabeth said.

"Me neither," Edward said. "But here it is, right in our hands."

They huddled over it together.

"I don't see anything that jumps out at me," Trinity said.

"No, wait, look at the edges. It seems there is something there. It is printed very small, but there is something there," Elisabeth said.

"Yes, I see it too," Edward said.

"It is too blurry to make out, so I will take your word for it. My eyes are too old to read anything that small," Trinity replied.

They noticed some people coming down the hall, and they realized they needed to take their discussion elsewhere. They went back downstairs towards the entrance. Trinity folded up the survey, and put it in her purse.

Chapter 14 Castle

Just as they walked out the door, Trinity remembered something. She had to get a copy of the certified death certificate from the clerk of the courts to take to the attorney.

"Hey, wait a minute. I need to go into the courthouse to get something," she said.

"That old, red, brick one over there?" Edward asked. "Cool, I need to go over there to look around."

"Then we will all go. I was going to ask if you wanted to wait in the car because it shouldn't take too long, but you can come with me if you'd like," Trinity said.

"Great!" Edward said.

They walked across the street and onto the elevated sidewalk that connected to the main door of the old courthouse. It was a very old, very sturdy looking building. If one didn't know, one would think it was built in the likeness of a castle. It was very large, and it took up what was the original block for the center of the town. It was surrounded by a stone mason wall. If there had been a moat around it, it would definitely have passed as a castle.

As soon as they opened the door to enter, they noticed the combined scent of archived documents and original building materials. The place was authentic, from its time worn marble floors to the original plaster trim.

"This place is amazing!" Edward said, as he stepped into the vestibule.

"It's huge!" Elisabeth said, as she looked around.

Just then a booming voice was heard, and a uniformed officer stepped out from behind a divider on their left.

"Can I help you?" a stern voice asked, with no inflection. "Where do you need to go today?"

Trinity stayed calm and said, "We need to go to the Clerk's Office to get a death certificate. I presume we're in the right place?"

"Yes, you are in the right place. It's down the end of the hall on your left, but you need to go through this security gate first. Please put your bags on the belt to be scanned. Do you have any knives, guns, drugs, or cell phones?" he asked harshly.

"Yes, we all have our cell phones, why?" Trinity asked.

"They are not allowed in the building, so you need to go put them in your vehicle," the officer said.

"Can we give them to my daughter, and she can go put them in the car?"

"It doesn't bother me what you do with them, you just can't bring them in here," he replied.

Trinity handed Elisabeth the cell phones and directed her to put them in the car.

"Then come meet us at the Clerk's Office," Trinity said.

Elisabeth went back outside to the car. The day had grown to be just perfect, and the sun beamed down on her back as she walked. She had the most unique feeling of contentment, and was sure Ida was still watching over her as she walked in stride.

She got to the car, and placed the phones in the compartment under the seat. She locked the car with the remote. "Beep, beep," the car chirped, as she pushed the lock button. She pushed it a second time to be sure. "Beep, beep" the car chirped again.

Satisfied that the car was secure, she stepped back up on the sidewalk. As she was walking past the buildings, she couldn't help but enjoy their facades. The old newspaper building, with its bronze plaque hanging outside, was really neat. The plaque appeared to be original to the old building, maybe as old as the newspaper itself. The headlines on the paper in the newspaper stand box reminded her of the articles she had read that morning when she got up. It wasn't anything she hadn't already seen, she thought.

She made her way back to the old courthouse, and checked through security without any problems. The officer seemed more inviting, and he told her that her family was still down the hall. She thanked him, and proceeded farther into the building.

The landmark was even more amazing on the inside. The sun was shining through the stained glass windows, all the way down the center of the building. The space was open above, and the ceiling was at the highest floor. The sun filled the entire space with warm light.

There was a very safe aura about the place, and it was quite welcoming to be in. The plaster nuances were a marvel to look at, and the stained glass windows were a sight to behold.

She could hear Edward talking in the distance, as she walked closer.

"This must have been something to build," Edward said.

"Yes, it's gorgeous, isn't it?" Trinity said. "I always forget how breathtaking this courthouse is when you get inside. It used to be the center of everything in town. All of the offices were in here. We always came here for everything county related."

The clerk helped them get the copy and certified it while Trinity was still marveling at the decorative moldings on the staircase.

"Do you think we could go look around?" Edward asked the clerk behind the counter.

"That would be fine," the clerk said.

"Oh, cool, let's go check this place out," he said.

They walked around to the stairwell, and held on to the railing while they climbed. They were amazed at the scroll work embedded in the stair rails. On the second floor, they took their time to circle the entire perimeter so they wouldn't miss a thing. The old elevator was next to an open door that looked like a vault. There were some people in there looking through the books.

Edward peeked in and one of the ladies saw him.

"Hello, can I help you?" she asked.

"Oh, not really, I'm just looking around. What is this, some kind of a safe?"

"Kind of, it is a vault for the recorder of the county."

"Really? We were just over in the Recorder's Office a few minutes ago," Edward said.

Elisabeth lightly pushed his arm, and he looked over to acknowledge that he was not going to say anything.

"That is our normal office over there where you just visited. This is the old vault that protects the original paper documents," the lady said.

"You say this is where you have the original sized ones?" Elisabeth asked, and Trinity lightly pushed Elisabeth's arm now. Elisabeth turned and gave her a look that said it was ok.

"Only the older, larger originals are here. The newer ones are scanned in and saved digitally," the lady said.

"We got a newer one, but the copy is so small," Elisabeth said.

"That's because we can only print that size of paper. The Surveyor's Office, over in the other building downstairs from us, can print big copies if you'd like," the lady said.

"Oh, is that so?" Trinity asked.

"Yes, they have a large printer."

"That's great!" Edward said, very excitedly. "Thanks so much for telling us that."

"You're welcome," the lady said. "Have a good day."

Edward turned to leave, and Elisabeth and Trinity thanked the lady in the vault. They finished looking around the building and decided to head for the stairs. On the way down, the three looked at each other. They knew they were thinking the same thing.

"We have to stop back at the Surveyor's Office," Trinity said.

On their way out, the officer asked if they got everything they needed.

"Yes, we sure did, thank you," Trinity said.

"Well, then you have an outstanding day," he replied.

They hurried back across the elevated sidewalk, and down the ramp towards the first building they had been in. Being more familiar with the layout, they walked right in the main door, and made haste into the Surveyor's Office.

The nice lady behind the counter saw them come in again, and got up to help them.

"You are back, I see," she said.

"Yes, we are. My name is Trinity."

"I'm Diane, nice to meet you."

"We want to know if you can help us."

"Well, I'll sure try. What do you need?"

"Well, we got this copy of a survey of my mom's house. We were wondering if there was a way to get a bigger copy."

129

"Do you have a deed record number?" Diane asked.

Trinity told her the number, and Diane wrote it down on a scrap piece of paper. She walked back to her desk and entered it in her computer.

"You're in luck. It looks like we have that one. I will make you a full sized copy," Diane said with a smile.

"Oh, that would be great." Trinity said, using all her strength to keep calm.

The printer behind the desk made some clicking noises, and a few seconds later, a large print came out of the top.

"Wow! That was fast!" Edward said.

"Yes, it's working really well today," Diane replied.

Another employee emerged from the back carrying the newspaper.

"Hey Diane, do you want the newspaper?"

"No thanks, I already read it today."

"Alright then, I will put this Herald Argus on top of the filing cabinet if anybody else wants it."

"Thanks anyway," Diane said with a contrived grin. She pulled the copy from the machine and placed it on the counter in front of Trinity. "Here you go," she said.

"How much do we owe you?" Trinity asked.

"Oh, there is no charge. We are glad to help. Do you want to roll it up or fold it?"

"Rolled is fine," Trinity said.

Diane got a small rubber band from her desk, rolled the copy up like she'd done it a million times before, and handed it to Trinity.

"Is there anything else we can get for you today?" Diane asked.

"No, this is perfect."

"Have a good day then," Diane said.

When Trinity turned around to leave, she bumped into Elisabeth, who was just standing there with a dead stare.

"Is there something wrong, Elisabeth?" Edward asked.

"I think I know what the other letters and numbers mean," Elisabeth replied. She pulled out the post-it note from her purse, and rushed outside and down the sidewalk. Trinity and Edward hurried to catch up to her.

"It's right in front of us!" Elisabeth said.

They found themselves standing in front of the building next door.

"It's right here!" Elisabeth said as she pointed to the bronze plaque, the one on the Herald Argus building.

"The Herald Argus, Grandma must have put something in the Herald Argus," Elisabeth said.

"It all makes sense now. She would have done it in the same trip," Trinity said.

132

Edward and Trinity were dumbfounded. "You've got to be kidding me," they both said in unison.

Trinity was so perplexed, she could only stand extremely still in one spot. The look on her face was clearly showing an out of body experience. It took her a moment before she came back to reality, then she turned to Elisabeth and Edward.

"We need to go to the library right now. We have to see if this is what we think it is."

"Great idea, Mom," Elisabeth said.

"The library? Where is the library?" Edward wondered aloud.

"Just a couple of blocks away," Elisabeth replied.

Chapter 15 Library

"Ok, cool, then it's another old building?" Edward asked.

"Yes, it is a historic building that has been added on to," Trinity said.

"Let's go! What are we waiting for?" Edward replied, as he walked in front of them to beat them to the car.

They drove across the main street, and turned at a one-way street that led to the library.

"It's right there on the corner," Trinity said, as they waited at the light.

"Oh, cool, find a place to park in front," Edward called from the back seat.

Trinity did a great job parallel parking in a spot exactly in front.

"Impressive, Mom. I would never have attempted that move with all those cars behind me," Elisabeth said.

"Oh, dear, it's not too hard. It just takes a lot of practice. It wasn't too long ago when there was a lot of parallel parking downtown, and that was the place we always went shopping, so I got good at it. It wasn't like the big parking lots we have now, where you pull in and back out really easy without worrying about people behind you."

"Well anyway, I am impressed, Mom. That was too cool."

"Actually, we do a lot of street parking at home," Edward said. "But that was very good. I am impressed too."

"Enough! I am getting embarrassed. We need to get inside to do our research," Trinity said.

Once out of the car, they were able to get a better look at the front of the building. The stone staircase to the front door was quite impressive. It rose to what was nearly the second floor, but it looked to be the main entrance. The front door was massive, and the detailing was from days gone by, when craftsmen were standard, and they took pride in their handiwork.

The door opened very easily and swung on its hinges with no effort at all. They walked in the main room which housed the front desk and reception area.

"How may we help you today?" the librarian asked.

"Hello, we would like to look up an old newspaper advertisement," Trinity said.

"Do you know how old it is?"

"It's about 10 years old," Trinity said.

"Then it would be on microfilm. It's in the room behind you and to the left. The microfilm is organized by date, and you will see the machines along the wall as you enter the room."

"Thank you," Trinity said.

They walked across the main floor of the old library, to the wide double door that said microfilm research room on the sign hanging above it. As they entered the room, they saw it was full of file cabinets, and the back wall had book shelves packed with very old and ornate bound books.

Edward noticed that familiar smell of historical relics filling the room. On top of a row of filing cabinets was a sign that read 'Archived Herald Argus Microfilm.' Edward saw it first, and led the way over to the bank of cabinets.

He saw that the fronts of the cabinets were labeled with a range of dates on each drawer. Before he was able to get the note from his wallet, Elisabeth had already reached into her purse. She had the post-it note in her hand, and looked to see if the date was the date of a newspaper. While she read it aloud, both Trinity and Edward scanned the drawers to see which one it could be in.

"Right here," Edward said. "It's in this range, in this drawer." He pulled the drawer open and rifled through the small boxes in it.

Edward located the box he needed and pulled it out. Elisabeth was already over at one of the microfilm machines to turn it on. Edward took the box over, and they huddled around the screen as Elisabeth loaded the microfilm into the machine. Without even realizing it completely, the trio was huddled tightly together to make sure no one else could see the screen, even though there were no others in the room.

Elisabeth pushed the forward button, and it whirred to life. It spun quickly at first, so Elisabeth let go of the button.

"Just a few more days forward," Trinity said.

Elisabeth pushed the button again, but this time she let it slowly scroll across the pages so they could see the dates run by on the screen.

"There, right there," Edward said.

On the screen was the front page of the newspaper for that day, but there was nothing special about it. They only saw the usual normal stories. There was a council meeting, where some things were passed, and some were not. They looked at each other and just shrugged their shoulders.

"Well, try just scrolling through the pages, but do it slowly. It would have to be a large story or an ad in the classified section with lots of information in it," Trinity said.

"You would be right," Edward said.

Elisabeth scrolled slowly and the pages passed by. Each advertisement was nothing out of the ordinary. They got to the classified section in no time. The legal ads were not anything special, but just as she got to the announcement section, they saw it.

"There it is! Oh my!" Trinity exclaimed.

"That is surreal," Edward said. "That has to be it. No one would have paid attention to it when she paid to have that put it in, but now we have it."

Elisabeth looked at it for a while, then lined up the page with the margins on the screen, and pushed the green print button. The machine cycled to print mode, the screen turned black for a second, then it returned to the page she had set. The paper was pulled from the tray on the left and came out on the tray to the right. Edward picked it up in amazement.

"You got it all on one page, and we can read it," he said.

"Nice job, Elisabeth," Trinity said.

"Mom, if you could go pay the front desk for the copy, I will put this back in the 'to be filed' box on top of the microfilm cabinet."

"Now, let's all just stay cool, and walk out of here quietly," Edward suggested.

Trinity paid the librarian, and they left without saying a word. They got back into the car and pulled out of the parking space into the oncoming traffic.

Chapter 16 Dad

As soon as they got to the stop sign, Trinity's phone began to ring.

"Will you get that for me, Elisabeth? I am driving."

Elisabeth found the phone in Trinity's purse, and answered it. The voice on the other end was a familiar one. It was Elisabeth's dad.

"Hello, it's your dad. Are you with your mom?"

"Yes, I am. She is driving, so she made me answer."

"I was just checking in to see where you two were."

"Well, Dad, we are going to be home in a little bit. Are you going to be home soon?"

"Yes, in a little while."

"We found out an amazing amount of things today. We need to run some thoughts by you to help us plan what to do next. On your way home, could you pick us up something to eat for dinner?"

"Ok, no problem, I will see you in about half an hour."

"Thanks, Dad, see you in a little bit then."

Elisabeth hit the end call button and placed the phone back into Trinity's purse.

"Dad is going to be home in a little bit with something to eat. We need to go over all this with him to get him in the loop here," Elisabeth said.

"I think that is a good idea," Edward said.

A few minutes later, Trinity pulled the car into the driveway. The garage door opened just in time for her to pull in. They all met in the kitchen, and put the things they had gathered that day on the table. Elisabeth grabbed a cup out of the cabinet, filled it with ice, and ran some cold water.

"Would you like some?" Elisabeth asked Edward.

"No, I am fine. Thanks though. Maybe when dinner gets here I will have some."

The round kitchen table was large enough to lay all the documents out on it. Elisabeth got a pen and a pad of paper from the den. Trinity got out the list they made at Ida's house, and put it on the table. They pulled their chairs up to the table's edge to look over all they had.

"Now let's go about this methodically. First we need to verify the survey document," Trinity said.

"Wait, we need to get a magnifying glass to read the fine print around the border of the drawing. We have to make sure we get it right," Elisabeth said.

"Yes, that would be helpful," Trinity said. "It's in the cabinet drawer of the phone desk curio, right behind you, Edward."

Edward turned and was able to reach the drawer without leaving his chair. He opened the drawer and fished around for the magnifying glass. The drawer was filled with papers, most of which were coupons.

"Are you sure it's in here?" he asked.

"Yes, that would be the only place I would have put it," Trinity said.

"Unless Dad took it out for something, you know how he is," Elisabeth said.

"Oh yes, I sure do," Trinity smirked. "Who knows where it could be if he had it last."

"No wait, here it is!" Edward said. He reached into the bottom of the drawer and pulled out the magnifying glass.

"Oh, thank heavens you found it," Trinity said.

Edward took the magnifying glass and scanned the document. "This works great. I can really make out all the words easily now. Boy, she was a wily one that Ida, wasn't she? It looks like she put a border on here herself after she received the copy of it. She must have either printed it out herself, or had it done by somebody else, because the text is tiny."

"Yes, nearly imperceptible," Elisabeth replied. All around the border, in the smallest font available, was a list of all the beanie babies and their type, all two hundred of them. The small text would not have been noticeable to the normal person. They would not have been looking for it, unless they knew it was there.

"I never thought my mom was that ingenious," Trinity said.

"She really went over the top on this one," Elisabeth replied.

"Edward, call out the text as you read it and Elisabeth and I will write it down on the list. Elisabeth, as he calls them out, write down exactly what he says, and I will do the same, so we can compare. We don't want to miss any of them.

Edward called out each one as he read. They were written in three rows, with a number separating each one. Edward was very careful to enunciate the best he could so it was very clear to Elisabeth and Trinity. He reached the last number and looked up. "Well that is it then. That was two hundred, right?"

"I got two hundred here," Elisabeth said.

"I do too," Trinity replied.

"Alright then, let's look at the advertisement next. How about having Elisabeth read that one and I will write down what she reads. That way it will lessen the possibility of me over looking items since I just read them," Edward said.

"Yes, that is a good idea," Trinity said.

Edward took the pen and paper from Elisabeth, and handed her the magnifying glass.

"You might not need this, but I am done with it for now. I am going to put a line down the middle of each sheet, to make another column. The ones Elisabeth calls out will go to the right of the ones I just wrote down. Then we can have a direct comparison of the two."

Trinity and Edward drew the columns neatly, and Elisabeth began calling out the list on the advertisement. They got through the list in no time.

"Number two hundred," Elisabeth said.

The three of them each looked at their lists to compare the items. Then they swapped, and carefully reviewed the lists again. They had to be sure they matched.

The sound of the garage door vibrated through the kitchen and they heard the car door shut. Tom walked into the kitchen with his arms full of brown bags of carryout food.

"I wasn't sure what you wanted, so I got a whole bunch of everything," Tom said.

"Thanks Dad, we are very hungry, but first you have to hear what we have now," Elisabeth said with sheer excitement.

Tom placed the bags of food on the counter and looked over to Trinity and Edward. He could see they hadn't even broken their stares at the lists they were holding. "I have dinner, you two," he said.

Elisabeth wasted no time and got out some dishes. She heaped them with food and placed them on the counter along with forks and napkins.

Trinity looked up, still completely entranced. "Thanks for getting dinner," she said.

"We really need to go over the magnitude of this, Tom."

"Ok, ok, what did you find that is so important?"

"When we went to pay the taxes for my mom's house, we figured out that the first set of letters and numbers was a reference to a document in the Recorder's Office. So we got a copy of it. It is this large drawing right here."

Tom picked up the drawing and looked it over.

"Then we were walking down the sidewalk and realized the other letters and numbers referenced a newspaper date. We went to the library and pulled a copy of the microfilm. Those are the other copies there on the table," Trinity said.

Tom's eyes lit up and he smiled from ear to ear. "This is a survey of your mom's house!" he said.

"Yes, and you should have seen the look on our faces when the lady in the Recorder's

Office put it down in front of us. We were completely stunned. It took all we had not to say anything and walk out quietly."

"I bet it did. I would have probably lost it. So where is the list from the drawing then?"

"Right there," Edward replied, pointing.

"Right where?" Tom asked, obviously confused.

"Right there, in the border. Can you see it?" Edward asked.

"Oh that is super cool. She hid it in the border. I would have never looked there," Tom said. He picked up the magnifying glass to take a closer look at the border. He saw that each one was listed neatly in a row. "Your mom," he said, looking at Trinity.

"Yes, my mom. She has always been a lot of fun."

"Oh, she was a real treat," Tom said.

They finished eating, and cleared the table to make room to lay out all the documents and lists they had.

"This is what I think we should do," Tom said. "We need to make one more list and each of you should keep a copy for yourselves. Elisabeth can go to the bank and make three more copies of her list, and put one in each of the three safe deposit boxes that are holding the ones we have already. Then we need to take some time and think about the ramifications of this whole scenario. We need to act deliberately and think about how our actions might play out. We need to make sure this unfolds in an orderly manner. In my preliminary thoughts, I can see how this may get out of control in a real hurry."

They all nodded their heads in agreement. Trinity got another piece of paper and transcribed the list onto another sheet as Tom suggested. Tom double checked it, and gave it to Edward.

"Hold on to this and keep it in a safe place," Tom said.

"I will. Thank you," Edward replied, and tucked the document safely into his backpack.

Chapter 17 Trails

The days passed quickly that next week. Edward spent his time researching on the Internet to find some short day trips around the area. He also spent time around the house, trying to bring some new life into the quaint home he enjoyed staying at.

The old, faded carpets needed to be replaced, though they weren't badly worn. He was quite adept at doing the job. He went to the home improvement store and picked out some nice blue pile carpet, with a thick pad, for the living room and den. It took him two days to do the work. He seemed to struggle sometimes putting the carpet down without any help, but he finished the job himself, and was proud of how it turned out. It brightened up the room and brought a fresh, new smell in to the house.

The next day, after putting the carpet down, he returned to the house, and opened the front door. He definitely got a rush from the smell of newness as soon as he walked in. There was a whole new ambiance in the home and it was almost overwhelming. It was as if the house breathed new life, just like the day it was new, when Ida had walked in the first time the day she moved in. He could sense the friendly, strong will of Ida, as if she were present, thanking him for all he had done for her cherished home.

Edward would take a day trip out to a historical place, and then take a day off to spruce up the little house. He found himself inspired by the places he went, and the colors of the leaves he saw persuaded him to paint the foyer a warm shade of magenta. It brightened up the entrance and created an inviting feeling that welcomed people into the home.

He would take advantage of the cooler weather to touch up the paint on the outside. He patched some places on the roof that had gotten weather worn. He aligned the garage door and fixed the squeaks in the rails for the rollers. He took time to clean and detail the car, and upgrade all the fluids in it.

While searching around the house, he found a tool box in the mud room, and used it to change the brakes and belts in the car. He was a natural at car maintenance and had it running like a fine watch when he was done. He could sense the car was happy too, because as he drove to different sites, the car seemed to purr along.

When he stopped at the local gas station, he always struck up a conversation with the person at the pump next to him, or the attendant, when he went in to pay. He was able to get the best tips from the people he met randomly. He found some old, abandoned railroad trails and the most inspiring old bridges that were hidden away down the uninviting trails. He saw that people had been down the hidden trails recently, but he hardly ever ran into anyone while on them. The car handled the sometimes bumpy trails with ease, and at times the suspension seemed to sing a happy song to him on the most daring ones.

He stopped in to see Elisabeth and Trinity some nights and Trinity always made him the best dinner. He could get used to those dinners, but he didn't want to make a pest out of himself, so he tried to be on a mission somewhere when they would call him to invite him over. Besides, he really liked to be out somewhere, just as the sun was setting, and especially when he was down by the river. It was so peaceful and relaxing when he was out searching for a hidden gem in the warm evening sunset.

It was one of those normal nights, but it felt so special, and he thought the food was the best. The dinner that Trinity made was super and he was very content as they all sat in the television room and watched their favorite shows.

In his mind he was planning the trip for later in the week, and would really like to have someone who knew the area go with him.

"So what are your plans this week, Edward?" Trinity asked.

"Well, I was going to go down to the old town of Lomax, down on the river. I did some research after the museum people told me about it, and it seems to be really significant. I looked it up on the map online and it looks really easy to find."

"Oh, yeah? Where is it?" Trinity asked.

"It's just east of the main highway and south of the river. It looks like it's only a mile or so off the highway along an old county road. The Internet said it was an old pumping station for

Rockefeller and at one time it was a religious retreat for a while. I am planning on going down there Friday."

"Oh, that sounds cool," Elisabeth said. "I am off on Friday. Could I tag along?"

"That would be great," he replied. "I would enjoy some company on this one because the map shows some homes in the area, so if someone went along with me, it would be safer."

"Pick me up early Friday, but not too early, and we can stop for sandwiches to eat on the way out of town," Elisabeth said.

"Alright, then I will see you on Friday. I need to get back to rest after all of this fine cooking," Edward said.

"Thanks for the compliment!" Trinity said.

"Thanks again for dinner. It is always a pleasure to come over and have some of your great home cooking."

"You are welcome, Edward. You two stay safe out there and if it looks dangerous, please don't take any chances," Trinity said.

"Don't worry, Mom, we will be fine," Elisabeth said, and gave Edward a mischievous wink.

Chapter 18 Lomax

Friday was a really nice day and the sun shone bright. It was a perfect morning and wasn't too hot out yet. Edward pulled the car out of the garage and down the gravel driveway to head over and get Elisabeth. She was ready and waiting for him to pick her up. They stopped at a local convenience store and Edward gassed up the car, while Elisabeth went inside to pay and choose some sandwiches and snacks to take along.

"I got us two sandwiches, some pop, and some snacks," Elisabeth said, when she came out of the store and got in the car.

Edward tightened up the gas cap and got in. "Did you get me some mustard?" he asked.

"Of course I did," Elisabeth replied. "We're all ready to go."

They traveled out of town and headed south toward the river. It took them a while to get to the south end of the county.

"I was researching on the Internet and I came across an old photo of the bridge that used to go over the river. I saw it was an old, steel trestle bridge, but when I came down here the first time I could never find it. I am sure it must have been replaced, because this bridge looks like the standard, cookie cutter, transportation bridge. It's so sad it is gone," Edward said.

"Yes, I remember the old bridge," Elisabeth said. "It was really neat, but it was not the best for a highway and the semi-trucks were getting taller. I am sure they replaced it with an open span bridge. They had to make sure no one ran into the top of it and then they would have to close off the road until it got fixed. They must have fixed it while it was still open."

"Yes and the loads were probably getting bigger too, like that one," Edward said. He pointed to a car with an 'oversize load' sign mounted on it. It was in front of a long semi-truck hauling a very large, white cylinder.

"What is that?" Elisabeth asked.

"It looks to me like a part of a windmill. They are the coolest thing in Europe and they are about that big."

"Those must be huge if that is just one piece of it," she replied.

"They are truly large structures. Maybe that was another reason they replaced the bridge with an open span. I do not think that would have fit under the old bridge," Edward said.

"You are right. We have been seeing a lot of those windmills in America lately," Elisabeth agreed.

"Well, there you go, another engineer who looked ahead and could see how even something like windmills could affect bridge infrastructure."

"There it is," Elisabeth said. "Turn on that county road to the left. That's the one you said it was on."

Edward turned east onto the county road. It was narrow, but in good shape. There was nothing down the road except corn on each side. It was like a cavern or tunnel of tall corn.

"We need to look for another road going north next," he told Elisabeth. "It should be a short drive, so keep an eye open."

"There it is!" Elisabeth replied.

The road was narrower than the last, and trees flanked both sides. They traveled down the road until out of nowhere appeared a drive on the left, at the top of the small crest of the hill. There was a large, black gate, with a metal centerpiece displaying the word 'Lomax' on it.

"Wow! Now that is really cool!" Elisabeth said. "I need to get a picture of that."

They pulled up to the gate and saw a gravel lane with grass growing down the center of it. "Well, should we go down there?" Edward asked.

"Yes, it looks ok to me, and the gate is open."

Edward edged the car onto the gravel roadway and slowly drove down the road. They were both tense and it was palpable inside the car. Soon they drove up to a stop sign that said 'warning low flying aircraft crossing.'

"Hmm," Edward said. "That sure seems strange to have low flying aircraft out in the middle of nowhere."

Just as they approached the stop sign, they could see why. There was a grass runway to their right that was really long and well mowed.

"Oh, cool," Elisabeth said. "That is really neat."

"Yes, too cool, but I don't see any planes, so I think we can cross," Edward said.

"Yes, it looks clear to me."

They drove across the grass runway and proceeded down the road. Soon they reached a point where the road forked in two directions.

"Which way?" Elisabeth asked.

"I don't know," Edward replied. "How about we stay to the left? It looks like it follows that old railroad bed, so let's go that way."

"Ok, that's a good idea."

They kept going and just as they got past some brush, they saw an SUV parked in front of a large, brick building.

"Look," Edward said. "We should be ok now. There is a government plate on that SUV."

"Oh, good, now I feel better," Elisabeth said.

They pulled up to the vehicle and parked next to it. They saw three people standing in front of the building and talking. They stopped and looked at Edward and Elisabeth. Edward got out and gave a jovial hello. The three people said hello in return and seemed to greet them warmly.

"Hello, I'm Edward, and this is Elisabeth. We hope we are not intruding, but we saw the gate was open. I found this place on the Internet and just had to come see for myself."

The three people smiled and nodded their heads. "Yes, you are in the right place," the older gentleman said. "This is the site of the old Lomax Station. These two are here because they are thinking about buying this place. They want to

164

turn it into a public park for all to come and enjoy."

"Oh, cool, do you think it will happen?" Edward asked.

"We don't know, but we are going to try," the pair said. "Well, we need to get going. We have another meeting. Thanks for meeting with us today," they told the older gentleman.

"Thanks for coming down. Give me a call when you find out more," the gentleman said politely.

"We will. Take care of yourself," the pair said, and they exchanged handshakes with the older man. "It was nice to meet you," they said to Edward and Elisabeth. "You are in good hands with him. He knows quite a bit about this place."

The two got in their SUV, and in no time they were down the lane and out of sight.

"Well, what do you want to know?" the gentleman asked.

"I saw on the Internet that this was an old pumping station and later it was a religious retreat," Edward said.

"Yes, you are right. I was just getting ready to lock up, but if you will follow me, you can look at the buildings."

"Oh, yes, that would be great!" Elisabeth said.

They toured the buildings while the man spun a great tale of the pumping station's unbelievable past. He kept their attention the whole time. He showed them all the buildings, and told stories about each one as he locked them up.

"I understand the river is very close to here," Edward said.

"Well, yes, it's just north of here. The old railroad bridge is still there too. Follow me and I will take you there."

The three of them walked down the mowed lawn to the edge of some tall grass. The gentleman led them to a small path, and a few steps later, the river came into view. There it was, a gentle stream flowing by with a soothing sound.

"Wow, it sure is wider than I thought it would be," Edward said.

"Yes, it is really nice down here," the gentleman replied.

"Can we go on top of the bridge?" Elisabeth asked.

"Sure, you just need to go back a little ways to the old railroad bed, and then you can get to the bridge. But be careful, the bridge is old, and the deck has some holes in it."

"Ok, thanks," Edward replied.

"I need to get back to the buildings to finish locking up. After you are done on the bridge, stop up on your way out and I will make sure the gate is locked when we leave," the man said.

Elisabeth and Edward navigated their way through the tall weeds until they reached the bridge. They carefully walked out on it. The old bridge showed its age quite apparently. The old railroad ties on top of the steel beams were weathered to the point that some of them had completely fallen through. Edward stepped across the railroad ties and made sure he stayed only on the ones that were on top of the steel beams.

Elisabeth followed him, but she stopped in the middle to edge her way to the side of the bridge. She sat up on the edge of the side guard beam. Edward looked back and was concerned she was too close to the edge, since the bridge was quite high above the river.

"Be careful!" Edward said.

"I will, but it's so pretty up here! I can see all the way back to the highway."

Edward realized he needed to go over to her to make sure she stayed safe. As he made his way to the middle of the bridge, he tried to step only on the most solid railroad ties. One section of a tie was a bit too soft, and he suddenly felt a sharp piece of steel penetrate his shoe and puncture the flesh of his foot.

"Ah!" he cried out. "What was that?"

His body crumpled and he nearly lost his footing on the narrow beam. He had to be careful to make sure he stayed on the deck without falling through. Elisabeth jumped down from the railing and rushed over to help him.

"Are you alright?"

"Yes, I think so. I must have stepped on an old nail or something. It hurts pretty badly, but I think I will be fine." He regained his stance and carefully stepped over the ties and beams towards the way back.

"Are you sure you are ok?" Elisabeth asked.

"Yes, I will be fine, as long as I stay off of it for a bit."

Edward limped back towards the buildings. Elisabeth stayed by his side all the way and helped him into the car. The nice gentleman came over, just as Edward closed his door.

"Well, did you get to see everything you wanted to see?"

"Yes, we did. Thanks so much," Elisabeth replied.

"I will follow you out and lock the gate when we leave. If you want to come back again and the gate is open, just come on down the lane. If I am here, we could talk some more."

"We will do that. Thanks again for showing us the place," Elisabeth said.

Elisabeth got into the car and drove back down the county roads and out onto the state highway. They reached the edge of town and Edward was still quiet. Elisabeth didn't know if it was because he was thinking about the things they saw, or if he was in pain from the injury.

"Are you going to be ok, Edward?"

"Oh, I am going to be fine. I just need to rest."

"You know that was a rusty piece of steel you stepped on. I think you need a tetanus shot."

"Oh, do you think I really need one?"

"Yes, you do. Why don't we stop at Med Quick on the way back to the house? It's at the hospital."

"Alright, that would be good," Edward said. Edward didn't want to admit it, but he was glad that he had Elisabeth to look out for him.

Chapter 19 Hospital

Elisabeth drove down the main street in town and turned into the parking lot of the hospital. It was easy to find and she followed the sign marked Med Quick Outpatient Clinic.

"Oh, good, there is a parking spot right there," she said. She helped Edward out of the car and through the front entrance automatic sliding door. The receptionist greeted them and gave Edward some forms to fill out to get him to a doctor for the booster shot.

"This is just normal procedure," the receptionist said. "We need the paperwork to get you signed in."

"Ok, thanks," Edward said, as he grabbed the clipboard and found a seat in the waiting area. He filled out what seemed to be a multitude of forms. Elisabeth found a seat next to him and grabbed a magazine to leaf through.

"This might take a while," Elisabeth said.

"I am sure it probably will, but I am glad to be in America because if I was back home, it would take ten times as long."

Edward used the pen attached to the cord on the clipboard to fill out all the forms. Elisabeth was reading an article in the magazine when a uniformed young woman walked by, glanced over at them, and then stopped.

"Elisabeth, is that you?"

"Oh, Melody! Hello! I haven't seen you in a while. Do you work here?"

"Yes, I am an x-ray tech," Melody said. "I got stuck in the Med Quick clinic this shift. I usually don't mind, but sometimes it seems, since I am the lowest tech on the totem pole, I get this shift more than I want too."

"Is it a long shift?" Elisabeth asked.

"Yes, if I am on this one, it is twelve hours. When it's slow, it seems like 20 hours. It's not too bad today. It is just busy enough to make the time go by fast."

"That's cool," Elisabeth replied.

174

"Hey, I see you are waiting to get checked in. Do you want a quick tour of the place while you wait?" Melody asked.

"Yes, could I? That is if you don't mind, Edward?"

"No, go ahead. I can fill out these forms and wait here. Just don't be too long," Edward said.

"Great, let's go then," Elisabeth said.

Melody led them down the hall and they passed through a door with a card scanner. They unlocked it and continued down a hallway until they turned to a room marked 'x-ray'.

"We can go in there?" Elisabeth asked.

"Yes, this is my area on this shift tonight."

"This place is really neat," Elisabeth said.

They walked into the room and Elisabeth saw another room behind a wall of glass, with some very expensive looking equipment in it.

"All of that in there is the newest high definition x-ray machine. We just got it a few months ago. It is so much better than the old one we had, that I trained on. This one brings out detail I never thought possible," Melody said.

"It looks impressive, but also intimidating," Elisabeth replied.

"Oh, yes, it can be, especially when we get the younger kids in here. When they are hurt, they are even more scared, so we have to be especially caring to them. It is intimidating to adults, let alone to fearful kids who are hurt and scared, because they have to be in this room by themselves."

"What do you do to make them feel safe?" Elisabeth asked.

"We do lots of things to help them. Sometimes we play music or we let them hold a stuffed animal, like this one."

Melody held up a beanie baby. Elisabeth was stunned at what she saw. The beanie baby had a blue ribbon on it. She was speechless as she looked at it. She couldn't believe it. It was right there, in front of her. "It couldn't be," she thought. "No way, it couldn't be."

Melody set the beanie baby down and looked at Elisabeth with a strange, quizzical look.

"Is there something wrong?" Melody asked.

"Oh, no, there's nothing wrong. I've just had a long day," Elisabeth replied, as she tried to regain composure. "So the toy helps calm the kids down then?"

"Yes, it usually does the trick. You know, we had a little boy in here once, and he was so scared. We tried everything, but he would not sit still to get the x-ray, and we really needed it. He had a broken arm, and it needed to be x-rayed quickly so the doctor could set it. We gave him the bear, and it took a while for him to calm down, but we took one quick x-ray. We had to try to get him back to his mom, but he was holding the bear so closely he wouldn't let it go. It ended up in the x-ray, so we had to take another. It was really strange because when the first one came up, the bear was in it, and there was a solid item in the bear that we could clearly see in the x-ray."

177

"Oh, yeah?" Elisabeth exclaimed. Her face lit up and she could hardly contain herself. "What did it look like?"

"I have it right here, in the saved file directory folder, if you want to look at it. I have looked at it numerous times and can't make it out. I can't tell you how many times I've studied it. Here I can pull it up for you." Melody pushed some buttons and the scan appeared on the screen.

"Wow that is so clear!" Elisabeth said.

"Yes, this new machine is really something. The clarity is amazing. I guess this is one of only a few in the country right now."

Elisabeth looked at the scan and could see the definite small outline of something dense in the image. It was a clearly defined shape and there wasn't anything else like it around it.

"How much definition does this scan have?" Elisabeth asked. "Can you zoom in on it?"

"Yes, we can zoom in really close. I haven't tried it yet, so let's do it," Melody said. Melody made a window around the anomaly and clicked the accept button. The scan zoomed in and they were both speechless for a second. "Do you see what I see?" Melody asked.

"Yes, I think so. I see something that looks like the shape of a diamond," Elisabeth said.

"Me, too. You mean to tell me there could be a diamond in that beanie bear?"

"It sure looks like a diamond to me."

"Oh, wow, this is amazing. How can it be?" Melody asked.

Elisabeth turned to Melody with the most sincere look and started talking.

"I have to tell you something, Melody. When you showed me the beanie bear, I saw it had a blue ribbon on it. After looking at it more closely, I see it is a special one. You see, years ago, my grandma made up this special group of beanie bears and put them out into society. She placed unique marks on each one and made a list of all the ones she made. I see this one has all the markers I know of, so I knew right away this is one of them that she did. But now you have

179

something I didn't know about, because my grandma never said anything about a diamond in them. The picture you have here clearly shows a diamond inside of it."

"I think so too," Melody said. "You mean your grandma made these and put them out so anyone could have one for free?"

"Yes, that is what she did."

"This is so cool," Melody replied.

"Now wait," Elisabeth said. "We just found out about this, so you know if it is all true and verifiable, this could be really crazy. So could you keep this quiet for a while until we can make sure it is real?"

"Well, I guess I could. You know this is huge, right?"

"Yes, that's why we need to be careful. This could be crazy, so crazy it would get out of control."

"Ok, I will keep it quiet," Melody agreed.

Elisabeth was overcome with the information and needed to get back to Edward, as she had been gone for quite a while. Melody walked with her back to the waiting room. They found Edward at the reception desk signing his release forms.

"Well, it was really good to see you, Melody," Elisabeth said, with the biggest sly grin on her face.

"Yes, it was great to see you, Elisabeth."

"I will be in touch," Elisabeth said.

"You better be," Melody said. "I will be waiting anxiously."

Edward looked at them strangely. He and Elisabeth walked out the front doors and Edward continued to stare at her.

"I will tell you in the car," she said.

"Ok," he mumbled.

Chapter 20 Dinner

They walked out to the parking lot and got in the car. Edward was quite tired and the pain had weakened him even more, so Elisabeth drove. They hadn't got but a few blocks onto the main street when her phone rang.

"Hello?" Elisabeth asked.

"Hello, this is Mom. How was your day?"

"Oh, good, and not so good. We went to Lomax and Edward stepped on a sharp, rusty thing. I made sure he went to the med center to get a tetanus shot. He seems really tired and maybe a little weak."

"Maybe he needs some good home cooking. I am making dinner, so how about you bring him over so we can help him get back up to speed."

"Ok, Mom, I will tell him we are going to our house for dinner. See you in a bit."

Edward glanced over to Elisabeth with his head firmly planted on the head rest. He was almost completely out of it.

"So, we are going to your house for dinner?" he asked.

"Yes, is that ok?"

"Yes, that sounds good to me. I need some nourishment to get back into gear. But you are going to have to tell me what was up at the hospital, when I am feeling better."

"Oh, I will. I need to tell my mom and dad too, so it's good we are going over there."

"Then let's make it quick, I am getting really hungry," he said.

They turned into the driveway in no time and went into the house. They went to the kitchen and the table was nearly set for dinner.

"Elisabeth, get the napkins and some silverware for all of us. Edward, you can sit down and relax a bit," Trinity said. Tom was there and already had the dishes out.

"It smells good!" Edward said. "What did you make?"

"I made a green pepper, cheese, and tomato casserole. It should get your energy level back up. I heard you had a long day," Trinity said.

"Yes, we did," Edward said. "I unfortunately got the worst of it, but Elisabeth took good care of me, and made sure I had a tetanus shot. But she was acting really weird when we left."

"Oh, really? Why was she acting weird?" Trinity asked.

"I don't know. I was waiting for her to tell me when we got here."

"Then sit down, everybody, so Elisabeth can tell us what she is so uptight about," Trinity said. They sat down at the table and Trinity served each of them a good meal.

"Ok then dear, tell us what you found out about today," Tom said.

"Well, when we went to the hospital, I ran into an old classmate, Melody."

"She was a good person in school, wasn't she? I never understood why you and she were not better friends," Trinity interrupted.

"That's a whole different story," Elisabeth replied. "Anyway, she remembered me, and she took me back to the x-ray area where she was stationed for that shift. When she brought me into the room, there it was, a beanie bear with a blue ribbon on it! I couldn't believe it!"

"Really?" Tom asked.

"Yes, and it gets better. She showed me the new high definition x-ray machine and that she had used the beanie bear to soothe kids who were frightened when they needed an x-ray. She had a recent scan saved on the terminal. It showed the beanie when it had once gotten in the way of the x-ray. It was unbelievable. The scan showed an anomaly in the bear. When she zoomed in on the area, it showed a distinctive shape of a diamond. It even showed the cut of the diamond to near perfect clarity because the new machine was so accurate. I had to tell her a little about grandma's beanies, but I told her to keep it quiet for now. I also told her to keep the bear very safe."

They were all listening very intently with a look of disbelief as Elisabeth told the story.

"Unbelievable," Trinity said.

"Are you sure it was a diamond?" Tom asked.

"Yes, I'm very sure. It was clearly distinctive and it nearly showed the clarity of the diamond. I could tell it was a round cut diamond at about a carat size. The only thing I couldn't discern exactly was the color, but I almost could with all the definition it brought out."

"No wonder you were so strange when we were leaving," Edward said.

"So, what do we do now?" Trinity asked.

"We need to calm down and do some investigation about the diamonds first," Tom said.

"You are right, we need to be certain there are diamonds in the bears, and that Ida put them there when she got them," Edward said.

"Good idea, we all need to check it out," Tom replied. "Edward, why don't you check around her house to see if there is any evidence of her buying any diamonds? We need to know what kind and where she bought them so we know if she did it for each bear. We need to be certain, because she left no clues in our other documents about the diamonds."

"How about we check this one first?" Elisabeth asked, as she placed the beanie on the kitchen table that she had in her purse. They all looked at the bear on the table, and were not sure how to react.

"Well, if it was my mom, she would have had to open up the bear somewhere to put the diamond into it. If she opened it up, she had to sew it back together again, so she must have done it by hand," Trinity said.

Elisabeth picked up the beanie and looked at it carefully for a few moments. "I can't see anything obvious," she said. "Here, you look, Mom." She gave the bear to Trinity. "You were shown how to sew by Grandma, so maybe you can decide where she opened and sewed the bear to put the diamond in it."

188

Trinity looked closely at the beanie. "Well, right here it looks like different thread under the left arm of the bear."

"Yes, yes, right here, you can tell someone did some work to the bear. I see it," Elisabeth said. "It's a completely different kind of thread."

"Then it looks like the ones we have, had been redone, so we should make sure there were diamonds in Ida's possession before we x-ray all of them," Tom said.

"Good idea, because if she didn't have the diamonds, who knows what else she might have put in them," Edward said.

"Trinity, you look at the rest of Ida's effects we have around here. Edward will check around her house. Elisabeth will look at the other ones at the bank to see if they have the same kind of thread under the left arm," Tom said. "We will get back together if anyone finds anything."

They all agreed to the plan, and then they helped Trinity clean up the kitchen. Elisabeth took Edward back home and made sure he would be alright for the evening.

Chapter 21 Jewels

The next few days, Edward cleaned Ida's house. He searched as he went, looking for clues about a diamond purchase, but he could not find any trace of evidence. He even checked the history file in her computer, but nothing seemed to point to a jewelry purchase anywhere.

Elisabeth went to the bank and looked at all the beanies in the boxes. She even looked at the one on the attendant's desk. Sure enough, they all had the same stitching under the left arm and with the same type of thread.

When she was leaving the bank, the receptionist saw her and wished her a good day. Elisabeth replied, "You too," but then she stopped and turned.

"Am I supposed to know you?" Elisabeth asked.

"No, but I remember you," the receptionist replied. "You are the granddaughter of Ida. She was the sweetest, most precious person I have ever met. She used to come in here regularly and we would make sure she was ok."

"Why would you say that?"

"Well, I say that because she would come in here and withdraw large sums of money, so we would make sure she always got back to her car safely. You know you can never be too safe."

"Yes, I know, but why would she withdraw large sums all the time?"

"We don't know, but we always thought it was because she was old school and wanted to make sure she had access to her money, since her parents lived through the whole bank crisis in the late twenties. You know, the older generation still can't seem to trust banks completely. We made sure she could at least get into her car safely."

"Oh, that was very nice of you," Elisabeth said.

"It was strange though, because after the security guard would escort her to her car, he would see her get back out and go across the street to the jewelry store. He kept an eye on her from afar, but she never came out with any bags of any sort. We figured she just enjoyed looking."

192

"She went to the jewelry store?"

"Yes, the one right across the street."

"Ok, thank you. It was nice to meet you," Elisabeth said, and quickly turned to go.

Elisabeth walked out the front door and looked across the street to see the old jewelry store. She thought about it a little bit and knew what she had to do. She went to the street corner and pushed the crosswalk button. The street was very busy and there was no way she was going to be able to cross without the walk signal. The signal changed and she crossed the street to the jewelry store.

She stood at the store front for a second. She felt a mystical feeling come over her. She could sense her grandma standing right beside her. It was the strangest, most melancholy feeling she had ever had. After a few moments she relaxed, and went toward the door. She grabbed the handle and pulled it open.

A bell rang out, as the door opened, to announce to the owners that a customer was there. The fragrance of an old retail building holding new products consumed her. The counters were filled with jewelry behind long glass showcases. The carpet was older, but well cared for, and it guided her toward the main desk at the end of the room.

A man came out from behind the divider and smiled at her. "How can I help you?" he asked.

"I am not sure," Elisabeth replied. "I understand my grandma used to come in here once in a while to look around, and I was wondering if you knew her."

"Well, you do look familiar. Are you the granddaughter of a lady named Ida?"

"Oh, yes! How did you know?"

"You happen to have a striking resemblance to her. I can see it in your face."

"Then you do know her! What did she come in here to look at?"

"She didn't just look; she came in here a lot to purchase a diamond or two. She always wanted a round cut, one carat diamond, but she wasn't too picky about the color or the clarity. I always thought it was strange, but who was I to question a nice lady like her. I figured she just wanted to have them, in case the currency collapsed or something. So I made sure I kept them on hand."

"How many times did she do this?" Elisabeth asked.

"I am not completely sure, but it went on for a long time. Sometimes she came in two or three times a week," the owner said.

"So, how many do you think she bought?" Elisabeth asked again, more intently than before.

"I am not really sure. Wait a minute, I can pull the docket of the receipts and tell you. See, I started to keep a separate file for her, just in case something happened to her or if she would have gotten robbed. Then she would have something to show her insurance agent. She could prove she actually had that amount of diamonds and the type, if she ever needed to get reimbursed for them. Hold on a minute," the owner said, as he disappeared behind the divider.

Elisabeth could hear the sound of a drawer opening and then closing. The owner emerged with a list in his hand.

"It looks like she purchased almost exactly two hundred of them," the owner said.

"Oh, I see. Is there any way you could make me a copy of that list?" Elisabeth said, as she tried to contain herself. "I can pay you for your time."

"It's no problem," he said. "It would be my pleasure. For all your grandma did for me, it's the least I can do."

The man made a copy of the list and gave it to Elisabeth. She thanked him immensely and offered him money several times for all his efforts, but he refused it.

Elisabeth drove home in a concerted hurry. On the way, she called Edward to see if he could stop over for a get together to talk about the discovery she had made. Edward was already parked in the driveway when Elisabeth pulled up. He was inside when Elisabeth walked into the house. They were all sitting in the parlor, drinking some lemonade, and eating lemon cookies.

Elisabeth thought it was weirdly funny, and the smirk on her face said it all. She went in and sat down on the small recliner. They all looked at her perplexed and then responded at the same time.

"Well, what did you find already?" they asked.

"Here you go!" she said, with authority, and she slapped the list on the coffee table, covering the stack of picture books of clocks and machines. Trinity was the first to move, and she dove for the list successfully.

"Well, what does it say?" Elisabeth's dad asked.

"It's a list!" Elisabeth said.

"We can see that," Edward replied.

"It's a list of two hundred diamonds that Grandma bought from the jewelry store. It tells the carat, cut, clarity, and color of each one," Elisabeth said.

197

"Whoa, are you kidding us?" Tom asked.

"No, I'm not in any way. I actually wish I was, because this brings everything to a new level. Now, I got this list from the store owner. He said Grandma was buying these diamonds two or three times a week. He wanted to make sure, if anything happened, he would have a list to give her so she could prove she bought them," Elisabeth said.

"Oh, my gosh," Trinity said. "This is amazing. There must be a quarter of a million dollars' worth of diamonds on this list."

"You got that right," Tom said. "This does bring this whole thing to an unbelievable height. Your mom was quite a wily woman," he said to Trinity.

"Yes, I am even astonished at her acumen on this one," Trinity replied. "She was quite a woman." Trinity gave the list to Edward and he looked at it very closely.

"You aren't kidding," Edward said. "There is over a quarter of a million dollars on here."

"So now we know she bought two hundred diamonds. We know she had two hundred beanie bears. We know the one bear at the hospital has a diamond in it, and the ones we have showed signs that the thread was redone on each of them. We don't know which diamonds are in which beanie, though. Other than a diamond in each one of them, that's all we can truly verify," Tom said.

"Yes, so what do we do now?" Elisabeth questioned very loudly. "This is driving me crazy! I don't know when another fun twist will come next. Knowing Grandma, she has more riddles to come, just like the last one."

"You can be sure of that," Trinity said.

"Now, listen, we go back to our original plan to lay low and think about how to proceed and react," Edward said.

"I agree, that is the best plan," Tom said.

"Fine, then I will be ok with that," Elisabeth said. "I just need a little time to unwind, and hopefully not run into another mystery."

"Me, too," Trinity said.

Edward was in deep thought as he got into Ida's car to drive home. Elisabeth, Trinity, and Tom went to their respective parts of the house to unwind. The list and the beanie babies sat on the table as a tribute to the remarkable adventure Ida set up for them. The evening hovered around them, and the still, night air was as quiet as it had ever been.

Chapter 22 Aukiki

The next Saturday, Elisabeth had recovered from the last find and called Edward to see what he was up to.

"Hello," Edward said as he answered the phone.

"Hello, I was calling to see what you were up to lately," Elisabeth said.

"Well, after taking these last few days I needed to recover from the diamond find, I am getting a little restless now."

"Do you want to go with me to a place on the Kankakee called Baum's Bridge?"

"Oh, that would be great!" he said. "I found a little bit about that on the Internet when I was looking for other information, so I really want to go there."

"Well, today is their Aukiki River Festival. It celebrates the old Kankakee River with some reenactments and people dressed in historical costumes."

"That is even better," Edward said. "I am in."

"Alright, I will pick you up in few minutes," Elisabeth said.

"Ok, I will be ready."

Edward got some of his printouts from the computer desk and gathered his keys and wallet. It only took Elisabeth a short time and she pulled up in the driveway. Edward went out the front door and locked it behind him. He got in the passenger side and placed the paper work in the center console. Elisabeth backed out of the driveway and they headed out of town and west towards Baum's Bridge.

The trip seemed to dance by in a very short time. Before they knew it, they were driving around some winding roads and it looked like they would end up down by the river very soon. At the last bend to the right appeared an old, tall, white building. It had definitely seen better days. Edward saw some signs that directed them to park on the left side.

"Over there," Edward said, and pointed to a parking spot in the grass. It was a nice spot right on the end.

Elisabeth lined the car up next to the others and they walked up the grassy slope to the vendor area. They were greeted with varying types of displays. They wandered about the fair and tried to take it all in. They watched iron smelters and yarn spinners recreate the techniques of yesteryear. There were many river enthusiasts dressed up in period clothing and all sorts of other revelers enjoying the scenery.

The air seemed heavy and the sound of the river flowing by was quite peaceful. The smoke from the various fire pits filled the air with an enticing aroma of food prepared old style. It made them very hungry and they were thankful when they found bison burgers and corn fritters to try. The food was fantastic. They drank sarsaparilla root beer while they strolled around and spoke with everyone they met.

Soon they had seen all there was to see, so they decided to head for home. They were walking to the exit when Edward stopped next to a table with a grouping of old pictures on it. One of the pictures showed a group of people getting their picture taken next to a young, regal looking man. In the background were a few large, military type outfits. Edward looked twice and it was exactly what he initially thought. The gentleman behind the table was sorting some other documents from a very old, weathered box and turned to see Edward and Elisabeth standing there.

"Hello," the man said. Edward looked up at the man and returned the greeting.

"Oh, I see you took some interest in that one," the man said. "That is quite the picture and it is the only one I have ever seen like it."

"This can't be what I think it is," Edward said.

"Yes, it is," the man replied.

"This is the Prince of Wales standing next to the locals, with his armed royal guard in the background?" Edward asked.

"Yes, you are correct. You know your history well."

"The trip to America was the first for the royal family since America sought independence. It went a long way in improving relations between England and America," Edward said.

"You are right, but I get the feeling that you are interested in more than that," the man said. Edward looked right at him and wondered how the man picked up on that. "I see you want to know something else," the man said.

"Well, yes, you are right. I was curious about the legend of the prince's true purpose."

"Oh, and what would that be?" the man asked.

"You know. The lost coin of Jesus."

The man looked straight at Edward, and then at Elisabeth, before he calmly asked, "The coin? You are looking for the coin?"

Edward sternly leaned forward and whispered, "Do you know of it or its location?"

The man looked at Edward with a wily smile and said, "Oh, you must be kidding!" His tone was suddenly joking and he chuckled. "I have heard a lot of wild stories about a coin of immeasurable force. Some say it was last known to be in the area. Some even say the prince was here looking for it."

"Well, some have said that," Edward replied.

The man continued, "If the coin was here, if there was a coin of that magnitude, then why, pray tell, did the prince leave? Why, when he returned to England, did his mother, Queen Victoria, send him to Egypt, Jerusalem, Damascus, Beirut, and Constantinople for a tour? She must have known old tales of a coin. If it existed anyway, his presence here in this area was a wild goose chase. She must have known or was told, the more likely place was still in the area of Biblical times."

"Well, I presume that would make more sense," Edward replied. "I did see that timeline on the Internet about the prince and his mother, Queen Victoria. She must have had better information then. You are truly knowledgeable about this history, are you a professor or something?"

"Why, yes, I am a professor at the local university, but in the Science of Archeology Department."

"Oh, that is great! You are from the university? You are exactly the person I needed to find. I am sure glad we came here and ran into you," Edward said.

"Why is that?"

"Well, I am from England, and I came here to look for clues to the existence of the mythical coin of Jesus. I would really like to come see you at the university sometime."

"Sure, that would be fine. I am usually around there during the week. Tuesdays and Thursdays are the best days in my schedule."

"I will make a point to come up there next Thursday, and I will buy you lunch," Edward said.

"That sounds good," the professor replied. "Then I could show you the newest technology we have for archeological investigation."

"Oh, yeah?" Edward quickly replied.

"Yes, it is an enhanced analyzer that can carbon date with increased accuracy. It will even analyze down to near molecular levels. It can find things like spores and pollens, and can help substantiate the date of the item with a very small sample size."

Elisabeth's eyes lit up as she turned directly to Edward. When he looked at her, he knew what she was thinking, so he mouthed the words, "No, not now." She gave him a sheepish look and backed down.

"Then it's a plan," Edward said. "I will stop in next Thursday."

"I look forward to it," the professor replied.

The fair was really going well and there were people everywhere, so they decided to leave. They walked past the old lodge, which was standing on its last leg, but the picture on the sign showed it in its heyday. It stood proudly next to the flowing river. The river was so deep it looked like a lake. The stream channel was much drier now, and it barely flowed by with a trickle. The place the picture was taken was now all full of foliage and vegetation, as if it hadn't seen water in decades. It looked very different from the way it did in the old black and white photograph.

Edward and Elisabeth got into the car to make their way home. Edward was looking at the map app in his phone, to see if he could figure out how the old river channel had gotten so dry. He could see a formerly large meander on the map that appeared to show the past outline of where the river meander had been. It was once very large, but now it was almost dry. It was quite a distance from the straightened river that now flowed past it.

"What a shame," Edward said. "The old river was cut off by the newly straightened river. We saw what it looked like then in the picture and what it looks like now."

"Yes, it is dry now. The river must have been quite a scene in its day when it ran at full steam. It probably flooded everywhere we were today when it flowed freely," Elisabeth said.

"I guess you are right. It would have been completely uncontrollable in its natural state, but maybe there is a way somebody could put some meanders back. They could be large enough to let the river fill them up and not overwhelm the surrounding land. The channel could be left straightened so that it could handle the high flow events."

"That is a good idea. I am sure with the technology we have today, somebody might be able to engineer that," Elisabeth said.

"Yes, I am sure they could," Edward agreed.

They drove down some of the country roads to find their way back to the state highway.

"What are those papers?" Elisabeth asked.

"These are a few places I looked up in the computer that looked really interesting," Edward replied. "Like this one, it's called Dogs Head Bridge, and it's down in this area. It has a long tale about it."

"Oh, I know that one! My grandma told me a little about it. It was a bridge over the Kankakee. A young couple was driving on it and they hit a dog and crashed. They never found the woman's body."

"Or the dog's head," Edward cut in. "So, they say she haunts the bridge now. She has a woman's body with a dog's head."

"That is so not believable!" Elisabeth said.

"We are really close, do you want to go?" Edward asked.

"Now? It's getting dark and foggy out!"

"Yes, now. It would be fun."

"Fun, you say? Not fun in my mind," Elisabeth protested.

"Oh, come on, let's go. We are really close," Edward begged.

"Alright, but I will drive, so if I get really frightened, we will turn back."

"It's a deal," Edward said.

They drove down the state highway and turned down a county road. They made several turns until they arrived at what looked to be the place. The abandoned road to the north was completely blocked with a barricade. They drove all the way up to it and stopped.

"Well, this must be it. I guess we have to walk from here," Edward said.

"Here? It's a long way and it's really dark out now!" Elisabeth said.

"That's ok. I will walk close to you."

"It's foggy."

"We can see quite a ways out and in every direction."

"Oh, ok," Elisabeth said trembling. "But if it gets really scary, we are going back!"

"Alright, Elisabeth," Edward said, and zipped up his jacket.

Chapter 23 Bridge

The fog hung over them like the damp blanket and the heavy air was still in the dead of the night. The look on Elisabeth's face was surreal, to say the least. She was not in control of her body and it was screaming at her to stay in the car or go back home, but somehow she moved forward with a robotic gait.

They had walked around the car and down the roadway until they came to a gate with a sign that said "road closed." The path around it was narrow, but it looked like it had been used recently, and they managed to get back onto the old, well-worn roadway. It was overgrown, mostly with grass, but was apparently a paved road a long time ago.

The veiled glow of the moon gave them enough light to guide their every step and every step was exactly that; a slow step by step walk down the old road. On both sides were farm fields with some crops already harvested on one side, while the other side still waited for harvest. The crops that were left and the remnants on the ground somehow rustled without any wind.

Edward and Elisabeth remembered the stories they read of ghost hunters going out there at night and recording strange lights and sounds in the distance. Elisabeth was completely set in her pace as she slowly walked in a concerted gait, with each step possibly her last. She struggled to keep moving forward, and she kept looking back at the car.

Edward stayed close and kept them steadfastly moving towards the bridge. Suddenly, a quick rustling came from the low brush next to them. Elisabeth jumped to the side, nearly pushing Edward off the old roadway.

"What was that?" she said.

"I don't know, but it was right there next to us," Edward said.

"Yeah, it was right next to me! You heard it, right?"

"Yes, I think it was a small rodent in the brush that we scared up because we were walking close to the nest it made for the night. It's cold out and it probably was in the nest keeping warm until

214

it heard us. It scurried out because it thought it was going to be hunted."

"Oh, I hope that is all it was," Elisabeth replied. "One more of those and I am going back!" she said emphatically.

"One more of those and I am going back too," Edward replied.

They continued on down the road a little farther. The fog seemed to gain density and each time Elisabeth looked back, she would lose more sight of the car. The night air was getting colder without any breeze of any sort. Elisabeth felt it only heightened her trepidation and she could not believe her body was still walking forward, but it was. She was becoming more curious than fearful, so she zipped up her coat tighter and kept on.

The roadway was straight in front of them, but the fields on each side soon gave way to large rows of trees. They were very large, and very old. Some trees were so near their life span it seemed as though they could topple over in the slightest breeze. One large branch was lying across the road and the path around it was narrow, but obviously used before.

The old trees flanked both sides of them and it even seemed they were closing in tighter around them the farther they walked. Somehow the moon seemed to give an eerie glow in front of them and their eyes had adjusted well to the low light. Edward closed up his coat tighter as the cold was chilling him deeper and deeper.

They heard a loud cracking sound under their feet and Elisabeth jumped to the edge of the road, and into the weeds.

"What was that?" she yelled.

"I don't know!" Edward screamed back. "This is crazy. This is really freaking me out!"

It took a moment for them to relax and calm down. Elisabeth looked around while Edward stood stunned in the weeds on the other side of the road.

"Oh, look at this," she said quite jovially. "It was a dried branch I stepped on. The noise it made when it cracked nearly sent me out of my skin."

"You? What about me? I thought we were goners! If you get ready to step on another stick, tell me, would you?"

She smiled at him and said, "Oh, come on, let's keep going."

Edward looked at her with a sly smirk. "Ok, I am still in. It's only a little farther up and we already came this far."

As they continued on, they saw that the fog in the west had broken open to reveal a harvested field and another large tree row in the distance.

The silence was interrupted by a blood curdling howl. Elisabeth stopped dead in her tracks and grabbed Edward's arm.

"This is so bad!" she said.

They heard another loud howl, coming out of the darkness, but this time it was in concert with other howling sounds.

"Oh, no, we have to go back now," Elisabeth said. "Do you have something to protect us?"

"No, I don't, but if it is what I think it is, they will probably be more scared of us then we are of them. It sounds like they are off in the distance." Before Edward could finish his sentence, they could hear the creatures of the night howling once more.

"I guess it sounds like they are in the distance, but if they are hungry, they will do what they need to do to survive," Elisabeth said.

"If the sounds get any closer, then we will high tail it back to the car. If they are too close, then we climb up a tree for protection," Edward said.

Elisabeth looked at Edward like he had lost his mind. "Are you insane? Climb up a tree? If those are wolves or coyotes and we are getting closer to their den, they will come at us with no reserve!"

"Oh, they are far away. We will be fine," Edward replied coolly.

They slowly continued on until the next few steps revealed a steel beam rising out of the ground and up into the low lying fog. They both saw it at the same time. Their step increased slightly as they kept walking toward the beam.

As they got closer, the beam morphed into a bridge surrounded by vast, overgrown foliage. The bridge appeared in all its glory, lying safely like an infant, in the flora that had cradled it for years.

The path down the center of the bridge was clearly kept open by recent visitors, and it shone brightly under the moonlight. The fog had weirdly and distinctly gone away from around the bridge, as if in respect. They stopped just at the entrance and paused to view the old, steel beamed bridge. It still showed its grandeur from the day it was first erected. The vines had grown neatly into and around the beams in a distinctly planned fashion.

It looked like a scene straight out of a scary movie, but to Elisabeth and Edward it all at once held an inviting and safe feeling. They had no fear as they continued their journey onto what felt like an old friend. The deck of the bridge was in decent shape for its age and nary made a squeak as they walked on it. The sound of a loose tension support rod wafted through the night air, but they were not worried. They could see the rod slowly drifting back and forth and it seemed as though the bridge was quietly swaying in the night.

They stood in the middle of it and looked out both sides through the steel girders. The moon was full, and they could see the fog lying in the old river bed. It stood completely dry and was full of vegetation. It was a very peaceful sight and they both had the feeling that someone was happy that they were there. They both sensed the gratitude for the respect they showed for the old bridge and the folklore it had. It was the closest thing to being in heaven.

Elisabeth was looking around and she walked to the opposite side of the bridge to see how it looked from that direction. She was very careful to watch her step and in one quick moment she caught a glimpse of something. An old shoe lay in the short grass that was growing on the deck. It was very old and it looked like the ones she had seen in photographs from the thirties. It was about ankle high and the laces were well worn, but they appeared that they held up well for their age and being out in the weather.

"One shoe," she thought. "That is weird." She bent over to pick it up. Edward was watching her and asked what she found. Elisabeth walked back to the center of the bridge and showed Edward the shoe.

"It looks old. It looks like a woman's shoe," Edward said.

"Yes, I think so too."

"Well, just put it right here, in the opening at the side of the bridge. It will look like someone was standing at the rail overlooking the old river bed from this side."

"That would be neat," Elisabeth said. She placed the shoe on the bridge deck and pointed it out toward the old river. They stood there for a while and relished the ambiance of the night and the experience of just being there. The cold was less noticeable while they were standing there and the moon shined brightly down on them. It only took a few moments for them to realize the aura and all of the magic that the bridge held for them.

Feeling content, they decided to head back to the car. They walked off the bridge and down the road a little before turning to look back at the bridge. It was easily visible in all its grandeur and they both felt at one with the sight of it. They went down the road towards the car and nothing seemed to shake them out of the feeling of acceptance that they got from the old bridge. They passed the tree row and reached the open fields without fear. They turned around a couple of more times to pay respect for all the bridge had given them that night.

When they got into the car and started it up, they just sat there in silence, with the heater warming them. They had that rare feeling that one gets a very few times in a lifetime; the feeling that everything was right in the world.

Elisabeth knew it was time to go, so Edward backed the car out onto the county road and drove towards home. The trip back was quiet and surreal. Neither of them said a word all the way back, but they both could hear what the other was thinking.

Chapter 24 Professor

It was noon on Thursday and Edward dug through his notes he had on the table in the den. He was piecing together everything he had found out about the coin since he had arrived. He sorted and placed all the potential leads into one file and all the researched or visited leads into another file.

As he reviewed each item, he logged it into his laptop. He entered the data into a small program he designed to track and predict his future search options. It was one of his most proud accomplishments, but one he had never told anyone about. It was, in his mind, his best chance to track down the coin. The program he had written was a code that had an artificial intelligence aspect to it when it ran all the information that was entered. It would search the Internet during its runs, and would try to link information together. He logged all the new information in and filed the documents away. The last document he had was the name and number of the professor at the college and he remembered he needed to call him before they met. It was the personal information he needed, that he could only get one on one, to put into his program. That type of information usually led to more leads once the program ran it.

Edward picked up his phone and dialed the number. It rang so many times he thought it would surely go to the professor's voicemail, but just at the last ring, he answered.

"Hello?"

"Yes, hello, this is Edward. We met at the Aukiki Festival. I wanted to see when you had time to get together."

"Who is this?" the professor asked inquisitively.

"This is Edward. I am the one who was interested in the Prince of Wales and the Kankakee."

"Oh, yes, yes," the professor replied. "I remember now. You are on a quest for clues to the whereabouts of a mystical coin. Well, it's good to hear from you. I was beginning to think I scared you off by being so blunt."

"Yes, I am not one to discuss openly the search I am on. Some people think I am crazy and some people look at me with suspicion."

"I see. How are you doing then?"

"I am fine. I was just going through some notes and realized I forgot to call you. If I remember correctly, you are on campus most days, and I can meet you anytime you are free?"

"Oh, yes, well you have impeccable timing. I am free this afternoon and I am going to be on campus until my night class."

"Great, I can be out there at around one this afternoon."

"That would be fine. Just drive into the campus and find a place to park near the Life Building. I am in the basement research lab. You can't miss it once you get to the basement. The lab room has a large white analyzer in the middle of the room."

"Alright then, thank you very much."

"I will see you at one," the professor said.

225

"See you then," Edward replied.

Edward took care of all his daily routines around the house. After he had a light lunch, he grabbed his keys, a pad of paper, a pen, and his phone, and went out the front door to the car to make his way to the college. He drove through some mild traffic in the middle of town, got out to the west side, and on to the open highway.

As soon as he went past the last subdivision of townhomes, he remembered he needed to call Elisabeth, since he was going to be on campus. She would be there for class, so maybe she could go with him to meet the professor too. He dialed her number and it wasn't but two rings later that she answered.

"Hello, Elisabeth, this is Edward. I am on my way to meet the professor that we met at the festival. He said he had some free time this afternoon. I figured I should call you to see if you wanted to come along with me since you are on campus."

"Oh, that would be great! I am on campus now and I just got done with my last class today. I can wait until you get here and then we can go together."

"Ok, I will meet you in about fifteen minutes then."

"I will be here. Thanks."

The drive was typical and went quickly since Edward took the back road to the campus. There were very few people on that road, so it was a nice, calming drive down through the back country. Before he knew it, he was in the parking lot searching for a spot. He drove around a few times before he settled on a spot. It was a little farther away than he liked, but he couldn't wait anymore as it was getting close to one o'clock.

He locked the car and walked through the parking lot to the wide campus sidewalks that led towards the Tech Building. He had to walk behind the Tech Building to get to the Life Building. As he walked, he thought to himself, "How am I going to find Elisabeth here on campus? We never decided on a place to meet up." He reached for his phone, but as soon as he was going to unlock it to dial Elisabeth, he heard her voice call out.

"Edward! What luck! I was just going to call you too."

"Oh, there you are! Good timing. I should have told you I set the meeting up in the Life Building basement lab."

"I figured as much. I was in the library, so I came out here thinking you would have to walk by here to get to the Life Building."

"Good thinking," Edward replied.

They made their way to the Life Building and went downstairs. It was not a new building, but they could tell it was freshly renovated. They walked down the hall and sure enough, they found the lab. It would not have been hard to miss. The entire wall was made of glass and inside one could see the large, white analyzer. It appeared to be a large electronic microscope with a sample platform of strange proportions. The door was just around the corner and it was open, so they walked in.

They saw an office on the right, with a large desk inside. There were many different items on it. Some were in boxes and some were on the tables surrounding the desk, and were in different stages of sampling.

"I'll be right out," a voice came from behind the analyzer.

"Hello!" Edward and Elisabeth replied.

"Ah, it's you two. I thought I recognized you. Hello again," the professor said.

"Hello to you," they replied. "Thanks for meeting with us," Edward said.

"No problem here, I am always willing to meet with someone to show off this incredible equipment. Thanks for coming." They walked over to the analyzer. The control panel was on and waiting for a command to continue.

"You are just in time," the professor said. "I was just going to do a run on this piece of paper. It's from an old manuscript. I want to verify its age and place of origin to see if it is truly as old as the curator says it is. We want to see if it came from the place they say it came from. If it did, then its value is immense."

The machine spooled up as soon as he pressed the continue button. An image appeared on the screen, with some other data in a chart on another screen next to it.

"Well, there you go then, that's how it works," the professor said.

"That's it?" Elisabeth asked.

"Yes, it is that quick," the professor said.

"That is amazing!" Edward said.

"All the time and waiting we did before is now done in moments, and with intense accuracy too. So enough of this, you came here to talk about your search."

"Yes, we did," Edward said. "I have been researching this for the longest time and I am always looking for more information to guide me in a direction I hadn't thought of before."

"Let's go over to my office. I have a file for you to peruse."

The three walked over to the professor's office. The professor went straight to a filing cabinet and got out a folder with some information in it. The folder was labeled "Caesar."

"Here is what I have so far. I did a lot of research years ago, but I got dismayed and filed it all away a long time ago. You are welcome to look it over and make copies of whatever may help you, but under one condition. If you find the mythical coin, you need to call me and let me analyze it in private, of course," the professor said. "I will promise you I will keep it entirely confidential because I understand the implications behind finding the coin."

"That sounds good to me," Edward said.

He gave Edward the file. Edward sat down at a table before he opened it to review the items inside.

Chapter 25 Thread

"Please excuse me for a minute, I need to check on the data transfer from the scan I just did. I will be right back," the professor said.

"Ok," Elisabeth said.

Edward was looking at the documents and Elisabeth sat down in the other chair on the opposite side of the table. A few minutes later, the professor came back in to the office and peered over Edward's shoulder to see how he was doing.

"How is it looking?" the professor asked.

"I have some of these things, but a lot of them are old. Still, this will give me a new direction to explore," Edward replied.

The professor looked over at Elisabeth who was sitting quietly and not too interested. Her backpack was lying on the table next to her. The professor noticed part of a beanie bear peeking out of her bag.

"I see you have a bear, Elisabeth. My daughter was so into those years ago. They almost drove me nuts when they were hot. We had to go get them all the time because she loved them so much."

Elisabeth just looked at him, and then she looked at her bag, and saw that the bear was showing. Edward abruptly looked up from his papers and saw it too. The bear was right there.

"Which one is it?" the professor asked.

"It's the fantasy bear," Elisabeth replied.

"Oh, that one was really sought after in its day," the professor said. "I like the blue ribbon. It gives a special charm to it. Could I look at it, for old time's sake?"

Edward looked at her strangely and she returned the look. "Well, I guess that would be ok," she said. She reached into her backpack and handed the bear to the professor. He looked at it intensely and an inquisitive look came over his face.

"Do you think I could take a piece of the thread and run it through the analyzer? I would like to see if it tells us the age and location of where it was produced. If I am correct, it should return a date of around 1997 and a production location somewhere in China."

The professor smiled enthusiastically as he spoke. Edward and Elisabeth both looked at him with a decisive look and agreed that it would be fun. One could tell they were both thinking the same thing. They wanted to know what the result would be too.

The professor went out to the platform and got some scissors. He snipped a small piece of a loose thread from under the bear's arm.

"This should be enough."

"Wow, that's all you need? That is a tiny piece," Elisabeth said.

"You had me scared when you said you needed a sample," Edward said.

"Oh, no, all we need is a tiny amount now," the professor replied. He set the sample on the plate and went over to the control panel to enter the parameters. "We will go for all we can on this one," he said.

He checked the thread's position one more time, then he went over to the screen and pushed the continue button. It only took moments and the analyzer began processing the scan.

"Hmm," the professor said. "It shouldn't take this long. This is a newer dated item that shouldn't take a lot of time to compute. Only the really old things take a while because it has to process back to the last carbon date. Then it cross references the known spores and molds file to verify the information. Let me check the system again. I have never had it hang up before, but you never know when it comes to technology of this level."

He pressed some buttons and brought up a task screen. "No, it seems like it is processing. Maybe it's just so new it doesn't know what to do. We have not scanned anything this new yet, so this should be a good test."

A few minutes passed, and the professor looked quite puzzled. He scratched his face with a questioning gesture. "Hmm, this should not be," he said.

Elisabeth stepped near to look over the professor's shoulder and she saw the screen flash. The image of the scan came up and the information opened on the other screen.

"There you go," she said.

"Why, yes, it did work after all," the professor said.

The professor and Elisabeth looked at it and were stunned. Neither of them said a word.

"So what does it say, you two?" Edward asked.

"This can't be possible," the professor said.

"Wow!" Elisabeth exclaimed.

Edward pushed her to the side to get a view of the screen.

"Oh, my!" he said.

"That's an understatement," the professor added. "Let me see. I can run more diagnostics to make sure this is correct."

He typed some commands and the computer returned a passing result on all the items. He brought up the scan again and they looked at it in amazement.

"Does that say what I think it says?" Edward asked.

"It says it is dated at around 10 B.C. and comes from the area we now know as Israel, and more specifically Jerusalem," the professor said in disbelief.

"Oh, you have got to be kidding me!" Edward said.

"No, I'm not. It seems to be testing fine and the equipment is all good. I have run samples of this timeframe and location before for verification, so the analyzer has the date and location in the database. I am truly intrigued here," the professor said. "How can there be thread of this magnitude from this bear you have?"

Edward looked questionably at Elisabeth, who returned a look of despair.

"Well," she began timidly. "This is a special bear."

She told the professor the story about her grandma, and naturally, the professor was amazed.

"But that still doesn't explain the thread," the professor replied.

"Yes, how can the thread be that old?" Edward asked.

"Well," she said timidly again. "My grandma did have this strange, old length of rope that I was given when she passed. I thought nothing of it, but I kept it safe because it was hers, and she told me to keep it safe."

"So your grandma had a length of rope and it seems it was from Biblical times? Hmm, interesting," the professor said.

Edward's face lit up with astonishment. "You have got to be kidding me!" he said.

"What?" Elisabeth asked.

"Oh, this is just so cool," Edward said. "Our long ago relatives included Simon Stone."

"As in the Apostle Simon Stone?" the professor anxiously retorted.

"Yes, I have been told it is the same Simon Stone, the Apostle," Edward confirmed.

"So this is a length of rope, as in the type used by a carpenter as a standard form of measure to build things?" the professor asked.

Elisabeth was left breathless. "Oh, that couldn't be! How could a length of rope still be in that good of a condition after that long and why would it be that certain length?" she asked inquisitively.

"You see, during that age there were no standards of sorts. Well, not like you and I know, but just local nuances in each community and especially in the poorer villages. People made their own things and the carpenters needed something to measure with. The easiest, most available way, was to use a length of rope. It was the local standard of sorts," the professor explained.

"I guess I have always taken for granted our rulers and tape measures."

"We all do, but long ago they only had limited means and used what was available to them," the professor said.

"So this rope you think is from, well you know, Joseph, and maybe Jesus?" Edward asked in quiet reverence.

"I would never say that in public, but between the three of us, I get a strange feeling that the answer is yes. There has to be something very special about this rope that would give it such longevity. It is beyond my scientific rational explanation," the professor said.

The three of them just stood there for a few moments in reflection of what they had just learned. The silence was deafening. They quickly understood that they had to go about their normal lives in order to think this one through.

The professor began first, "I think we realize what we have here. If you still have that length of rope, you are always welcome to bring it back here and we will discreetly document it. We can see if it can lend us any more clues, other than the data we already have. I promise you, just like I promised to Edward, that I will truly keep this in the strictest confidence, no matter what."

Edward looked at Elisabeth as she said, "Yes, we will think about that, but it might not be for a while though."

"That's alright with me," the professor replied. "I will be around here whenever you are ready."

"I can't thank you enough," Edward said. "This is truly amazing and more than I ever thought it could be."

"You are quite welcome," the professor said.

"I need to get going home now," Elisabeth said.

They all parted ways in a quiet, stoic sense. Elisabeth and Edward drove home, while the professor took the data and secured it digitally. He shut down the lab and made sure the information was safe before he left the building for the evening.

Chapter 26 Melody

The day was extremely quiet and Melody was working the long shift as her turn required. She knew a quiet shift surely meant something would always spring up to make it interesting. The saying around the urgent care wing was "in like a lamb and out like a lion." Sometimes, she would want something to come up, as long as it wasn't too serious, so it would make the time go by faster.

The staff was taking their break. They were sitting around the break table knowing that something was bound to come up soon. The only thing in question was the severity of the situation. It seemed the longer a shift went with nothing major happening, the more severe the problem would be.

Melody was very happy that her turn was near the end because she wasn't scheduled for another two weeks. They sat around the table, eating snacks, and talking about the news of the day.

The police scanner crackled and they all stopped immediately. They instinctively turned to the scanner, as if they were expecting to see something on a display, but the scanner went quiet. They returned to what they were doing, and smiled at each other.

"Whew, I thought that was the call," the nurse said. The others nodded in agreement.

"Wait for it," an assistant said. "They always come in twos. Wait for it."

Then it came, first the crackle of the microphone keying up, and then the call. It was a 911 call for assistance. The call asked for an ambulance because a small child was choking. The child was breathing, but still choking severely. Dispatch gave the address and the paramedics were on their way.

"TEA three minutes," the paramedic said over the scanner.

They could hear the sounds of sirens over the speaker and they all knew what to do. They rushed to their stations and prepared for the arrival. It wasn't but a few minutes, though it seemed to pass in seconds, that the ambulance pulled up, and brought the child into the emergency room.

The paramedics bypassed the check in desk and went right into an observation room. The child had barely a pinkish skin tone and her breathing was low and heavy. Melody was in the hall and could see, through the open door, the nurses and the doctor trying desperately to help the child. She had swallowed something and it was lodged tightly in her throat. She could breathe, but it was getting worse every minute. Her mother was holding back a groundswell of tears, trying to be strong and calm for her daughter.

They tried every procedure they knew of, but to no avail. The eldest doctor had seen enough and ordered the child into the x-ray lab. He wanted to see what was lodged in her throat so tightly.

The little girl was frightened to no end and she could barely breathe. She was conscious, but her heart rate was such that they feared she would hyperventilate and pass out, so they had to act fast. They moved her into the x-ray room. Her mother

245

had to let her go, but just as she put her in the support chair, the little girl became extremely frightened and began shaking. It looked like she would surely take a turn for the worse.

There was no way she could get enough air with the item lodged in her throat. Melody recognized this and in a flash she emerged from behind the technician's wall with the beanie bear in her hand. The little girl grabbed the bear tightly and started to calm down.

Melody knew exactly what the bear could do. The little girl held the bear so tightly to her chest that Melody could barely get her seated in the chair properly for a good scan. The little girl became calmer and pressed the bear tightly to her chest. Melody saw her chance and rushed to the controls. She took the scan quickly.

The scan worked and the digital image showed up immediately. The doctor looked at it when it refreshed on the screen. He shook his head and rubbed his hand over his face.

"Oh, my," he said. "This is really bad. It's lodged really tight in a place we can't attempt to get to. It will cause mortal danger if we even try.

She can just barely breathe right now, so we have to find another way. Is there a way you can get me a scan from another angle?" the doctor asked Melody.

"Yes, I can see if she will twist a little to the side, since she has calmed down nicely now."

Melody went into the room and saw that the little girl was very still and calm. Out of the corner of her eye, she could see the girl's mother. She had also calmed down and looked a little less nervous. Melody knew the little girl's mother was at one with her daughter at that moment.

Melody tried to get the girl to move a little to the side. When she touched her arm, she could tell the little girl was holding on to the bear so tightly that every muscle in her body was severely strained. Melody became gravely concerned. The girl turned and looked at her with her large, hazel eyes that were still wet with the tears that now rolled down her cheeks.

Then she coughed. It was a low, heavy cough. Melody froze and wondered if she swallowed it, or if it had lodged tighter in her throat. The little girl convulsed forward and coughed heavily again, but this time she heaved strongly, and something fell out of her mouth.

Melody, still frozen, looked into the girl's eyes for a brief moment. Then the little girl smiled wide and her eyes slowly blinked. Melody was ready for anything that could have happened next.

"Thank you so much. I think it is gone now," the girl whispered. Then she breathed deeply and her normal color returned to her face and arms.

Melody went to hold her and could feel her muscles were at ease. The girl was finally in a peaceful state. Melody asked her if she was alright and she shook her head yes. She asked the girl if she would like to lie still for one moment longer before her mother came in. The girl gave Melody a warm, reassuring look, and said yes again.

Melody rushed over to the controls and hit the scan button quickly. The scan came up on the screen and she could see that the object was gone. The doctor took a look and confirmed it.

The doctor motioned to the girl's mother that it was alright for her to go in and comfort her daughter. He went into the room to pick up the item the girl coughed up. It was a small toy she must have been playing with. The shape of it was so odd, that he could not even begin to see how he would have been able to extract it easily.

The girl's mother, who was holding her daughter tightly, had tears in her eyes as she thanked all of them over and over again. The staff gathered in the room and began clapping out a round of applause to show respect to their fellow professionals.

Melody went to the girl, gave her a hug, and kneeled down in front of her. The little girl looked at Melody and said, "Thank you for letting me hold the bear. I held it as tight as I could. I knew it would help me. I just knew it was a special bear."

Her mother looked at her as she said this and knew she was happy and content now.

"You are right, that is a very special bear. We need to keep it here to help other kids just like you, so they can feel safe. The bear needs to stay here to watch over the other kids," Melody said.

The little girl was dismayed when she heard that, but she knew Melody was right. She opened her arms to give the bear back to her. The mother was so proud to watch her daughter hand it back to Melody. Before the little girl let go of the bear, she gave it a kiss on the top of its head and said, "Thank you, bear."

Everyone was extremely joyful and teary eyed. They all hugged the little girl and her mother as they left the observation room. Melody wearily found the couch in the staff break room, and collapsed into the cushions.

"Oh, what a way to end a shift," she said out loud. She lay on the couch in complete exhaustion. The doctor looked in on her and could tell she needed to be left alone.

"You did a great job, Melody. Thank you," the doctor said.

"You're welcome," she said, and closed her eyes.

Chapter 27 Mother

The next day, a reporter came by to talk to the hospital employees. He was looking for a feel good story about the saving of the little girl and he talked to everyone who was there. The reporter learned from the staff about the beanie bear the little girl had, and how heroic Melody had been. Melody gave the reporter an interview. She told him how the bear was a great comfort for all the distressed children who came into her department in time of need.

The story ran in the local paper the next day and in the regional news the following day. Everywhere Melody went, people thanked her for all she did. Melody would just say thanks and tell them she was just doing her job the best her talent afforded her. A few days went by and the little girl's mother stopped in to see if Melody was working. The receptionist rang Melody in the staff room. When Melody came out from the back through the swinging doors, her face lit up. She recognized the woman immediately and they embraced. Melody sat down with her in the waiting room.

"Well, I came here to talk to you about that comforting bear you have and to thank you again for all you did for my daughter. It was more than can be explained. The only way I can understand it, is to think of it as a miracle."

"Oh, no, it was just meant to be," Melody said smiling.

"I really want to talk to you about the bear though," the mother said.

Melody was worried and said, "We need to go in the back for a minute." They went to a small waiting area and Melody asked the mother, "What do you want to know about the bear?"

"Well, I was hoping you could let me have, or let me buy, the bear, so I can give it to my daughter," the mother said.

"Oh, I could never do that," Melody replied. "I understand your plight, but this bear has to stay here. There is no price high enough to ever let this bear leave here, after all it has done and will do for the scared patients who come in here. You see, this bear is very, very special."

"It is special to me!" the mother interrupted.

"No, you don't understand," Melody continued. "This bear is super special. You see, this bear has a diamond in it, and it is very rare."

"You mean they had diamond bears as collectables?" the mother asked.

"No, this bear is rare. I know it because it has a real, one carat diamond in it. Follow me and I will show you." Melody led the mother to the x-ray area. "See this scan here?" Melody asked, as she pressed the buttons and moved the mouse over to a folder to bring up the scan. "You see? Right there is the scan of the bear showing a diamond in it."

"Oh, I see! That means that bear is worth a whole lot of money just because the diamond is in it," the mother said.

"Yes, but there is more to it because there are more bears out there like it. They are extremely rare, and no one knows where they are. They could be anywhere."

"But I really need to do something," the mother said. "My daughter really needs some sort of bear to help her feel safe and secure now. It reminds her of the time she was saved."

"I am sure we can find something else. Let's look on the auction site to see if there is a twin of the same bear on there. You know, they made a lot of these beanie bears. I am sure there is one out there you could buy and put a blue ribbon on and give to her," Melody said.

"That would be great luck to find one of those bears. That bear was in high demand when it came out because there were not that many of them," the mother said.

"Oh, don't be a doubting Thomas!" Melody said. "I am sure we can find something online. Let's just look and see."

Melody logged in to the Internet and searched for the auction site. As soon as it came up, Melody typed in the description of the bear and clicked the search button. The computer flashed a new screen and some search results came up in a list.

"Ok, let's see what we have," Melody said. She scrolled down the list. Each one was close, but not exactly like the one she had. Melody was getting fearful they wouldn't find one and if they did, it would be expensive and far away. The bottom of the screen scrolled up and there it was; the exact same bear. They were both stunned and could barely look away from the screen. Then Melody saw something else. She gasped loudly and the mother looked at her.

"Are you alright?" she asked.

"Yes, look there," Melody said as she pointed to the screen.

"Oh, my! It can't be!"

"Yes, it can be," Melody said. "It's right here in town, just down the road at a resale shop. They only want a few dollars for it and they will ship it."

"Ship it?" the mother exclaimed. "I am going to get it right now!" The mom whirled out of her chair, her purse swung out around her, and she was gone through the door in no time.

255

Melody didn't know what had just happened and she looked at the vacant seat with amazement. "Wow, that was fast. She left out of here like white lightning. Amazing," Melody thought. Melody closed all the websites and logged off the computer. She needed to get back to her duties for the rest of the day.

Chapter 28 News

The sun was shining brightly and Edward was amazed at how warm the temperature was for being so far north. It was late in the year and warmer than it usually was. With the gusty winds and the warmer temperatures, Edward knew the weather was going to change shortly.

Edward was waiting at the stoplight and thinking the traffic was heavier than normal that afternoon, but he easily let it flow off his conscience, because he didn't have anywhere to go especially. He waited patiently while the radio played the same pop songs they played in what seemed like a daily loop. He was not interested in hearing the song over again, so he thought he would try to see what radio stations Ida had programmed into the car radio. He pushed the station button number four and it changed to a local radio station.

"This next segment is sponsored by your downtown furniture store. They've been a family owned business for over seventy-eight years serving all of your furniture needs. So visit your downtown store and support your local business," the radio jockey said. "And now, back to our show. Today, in the final segment of the local news, we have a story of a young child who was choking severely. After the hospital staff had nearly given up trying to remove the swallowed toy, the girl suddenly dislodged the hazard on her own, and is now fine. It's a local story of how precious life is. We are going to have her mother on our lunchtime local guest show tomorrow. She will tell us how grateful she is for all those who helped. So listen in tomorrow to hear the story of a small miracle, right here at our local hospital. Now back to the oldies afternoon show."

Edward was intrigued by what he heard. He kept the radio station on the rest of the way home to enjoy the old songs he knew Ida must have liked listening to.

It was a little past noon the next day and Trinity was running errands around town on her day off. She always looked forward to those days off during the week. She could get all her errands done during normal business hours when there were usually less people around. She was in between places when she turned on the radio. She wanted to catch up with local events on the local station. As soon as she put on the radio, she heard the announcer asking someone a question.

"So, you were in the emergency room then, with your daughter, and you were staying very calm for her? She was almost in a state of shock and could barely breathe, correct?"

"Yes, and the doctors and nurses were at their wits' end. They knew they could not go into her throat and dislodge it or they would have caused immense damage. She could have lost her ability to speak."

"Oh, my, then what happened?" the announcer questioned.

"Well, they took her into the x-ray room to get a look at it under this new, super powerful scanner. They took her into the scanning room and she was getting more and more afraid. I could sense it, but I knew I had to be strong. This nice technician helped her into the chair for the scan. She was about to hyperventilate. I could see that the technician could sense she had to do something, so that nice young lady gave her a beanie bear to hold. It had a blue ribbon on it and my daughter held it tight. I could see from the doorway she was holding onto it tighter than I have ever seen her hold anything. I was frightened that she was going to pass out gripping it that tightly, but I had to stay out of the room. The technician ran quickly to take the scan. As soon as she took it, my daughter coughed and coughed until the toy dislodged and she spat it out. It was amazing. She immediately turned a healthy hue and I knew she was alright."

"Did they let you go back in to be with her after that?"

"No, they had to take another scan to make sure the airway was free. Afterward, they let me go over to her. I held her so tightly. I told her everything was alright. When she looked at me and said, 'I know, Mom. Thank you,' I knew she was ok. She had that bear in her arms and I could sense a sort of static energy as the bear brushed against my arm. It was not the normal static energy. It was a deeper, stronger feeling. My daughter seemed to sense the same thing."

"So, you think the bear helped her out?" the announcer asked.

"Yes, I know the bear had something to do with it. I went back to the hospital and met with the technician to see if they would sell me the bear, so I could give it to my daughter, but she said she could not sell it to me. She said it was a very special bear, because it had a diamond in it, and it was extremely rare."

"They have a diamond bear down at the x-ray lab?"

"Yes, and it seems to be very special, well, at least very special to us. I think it saved my daughter's life!"

"Well, that is more of a story than I could have ever imagined for this show," the announcer said. "You heard it here, folks, the story turns now to a diamond bear with a special aura, right here in our own town. We only have a few moments left in the show, so could you tell us, was there anything special about this diamond bear?"

"No, it was a normal bear, except it did have a blue ribbon around its neck."

"I hate to stop you there, but we are out of time for today's local guest noon show. We now

261

have to go to our sponsors. Thank you for coming on the show today. We really need to have you back again soon."

Trinity was stunned to no end and had to pull over to decide what to do. "Oh, my, this is really happening now," she thought. She grabbed her phone and dialed her husband.

"Hello," he said immediately.

"Did you hear the radio show just now?" Trinity asked.

"Yes, I was listening. I can't believe it. The story is really out there and everybody just heard it."

"Yes, we need to act now," Trinity said.

"You are right. Get a hold of Elisabeth and have her call Edward. Have them meet at our house immediately. I will see you at home."

"Alright, I will call her," Trinity said.

Trinity called Elisabeth and told her what to do. It wasn't but forty-five minutes later that they were all gathered at home. Elisabeth was the last to arrive. When she walked in, her phone was beeping repeatedly, over and over again. She was extremely flustered and rushed in to the kitchen.

"Is that your message notification making that noise?" Edward asked.

"Yes, it has been going off non-stop for the last fifteen minutes. Those alerts are my social site status updates coming from my friend Melody's page. We added each other to our friends list after that time we were in the urgent care center with you. Her updates are blowing up my phone! What is going on?" Elisabeth exclaimed.

"Well, the noontime local guest show on the radio let the cat out of the bag. A lady on the show told everyone about a beanie bear with a diamond in it and a blue ribbon around its neck," Trinity said.

"What?" Edward shouted. "You have got to be kidding!"

"No, we are not kidding," Tom said. "I heard the show. This is happening right now."

"Oh, no, that's why Melody's social page is out of control," Elisabeth said.

"Yes, she is going to be involved in this now," Trinity said.

"What do we do?" Edward asked. "We have to get out of here."

"Yes, I know. Here is what we do. Edward, you go back and grab a suitcase to put some things in for an extended stay. Elisabeth will call you and tell you the address after Tom confirms the fact we can go there. Then you put the directions into your map application on your cell to get you there. It's a little tricky to find, but you should get there without any problems," Trinity said.

"Ok, I will do that," Edward replied.

"Tom, you call up your fishing buddy and ask him if we can stay at his cottage on the lake up in the north part of the county. You know the one, the lake near the rest area with the fast food place in it," Trinity said.

"Yes, I can call him. That should be fine because he is already down in Florida for the winter. I am sure he will be agreeable to that," Tom said.

"Elisabeth, you call your friend Melody and tell her you will call her in the next few days to try and help her deal with this whole situation. I will go next door to ask our neighbor to watch over the house and not let anyone on the property," Trinity said.

"Make sure she understands that nobody is allowed on the property," Tom said.

"Yes, I will make sure," Trinity replied. "Now, let's get going."

Chapter 29 Cottage

They all packed an extended stay suitcase and drove separately to the cottage. Edward got the address from Elisabeth and followed the directions on his phone. He drove out east of town, along an older state highway. The scenery was beautiful. The GPS directed him to turn off onto a county road that angled off the state highway at a smooth transition. It was not a perpendicular angle like most roads, and it appeared to be a very old state road.

He traveled north through some farm fields. He noticed the fields were very rolling and not wide open and flat like the other ones he was used to. The fields were smaller, but they were quite picturesque to look at while he drove. He came to a winding stretch of road that seemed to wind down the hill up ahead of him. He slowed down since the roadway was flanked by large, old trees that made the pavement seem narrower than it really was. Most of the curves he couldn't see around, so he needed to be careful about oncoming traffic.

He drove until he reached the lowest point on the road, and he could see the lake. It was magnificent. It was crystal blue and astonishing to look at. It was not the biggest lake he had ever seen, but it was peaceful in its own way.

He found the turn the GPS told him to take and he wound along some narrow roads. There were cottages on each side. He drove until the GPS told him he had arrived at his location. The cottage was a good size, but he could tell it had been added onto several times from its original, small footprint. It now looked like a very nice house. He parked to the left of the other cars and was part way into the grass. The parking area was definitely not large enough for a sizable crowd. The front entrance had a nautical motif of fishing nets and rope. They looked like they came from some large ocean going vessels and appeared to be well cared for. He tried the door, and it was unlocked, so he walked in.

The rest of the family was all there sitting around the great room table discussing the next plan of action. They needed to know more about how far the story had gone in the media. They knew they had to try to keep things under control.

Tom got up from the table to greet Edward when he walked in.

Edward could see that the cottage had been upgraded to the max. There was heating and cooling added along with all the electrical upgrades. It was wired for Internet and satellite television. There were also three bedrooms added on recently.

"So, this is a really nice fishing shack," Edward said.

"Oh, yes," Tom replied and smiled. "My buddy, Don, has been upgrading this for years. You see, as he got older, he tended to not to want to rough it so much, or maybe it was his wife's doing. They wanted the grandkids to come up and spend some time with them. You know kids these days, if they don't have their own bedroom with heating, cooling, and Internet, getting them to the cottage would be like pulling teeth. Don had the extra time to fix it up since he had retired. I helped him once in a while and it was always relaxing to come up here."

"Yes, I see that now," Trinity quipped. "I know you wouldn't spend that much time up here with Don if it was not really nice."

"You are right. Don made the place fun and relaxing. The lake is magnificent," Edward said. "It is almost surreal how blue the water is."

"Well, that is because it is spring fed and very deep in spots, so it stays quite blue. The lake is so clean that it is one of the few lakes in the world that has jellyfish in it," Tom said.

"Jellyfish?" Edward asked.

"Yes, they are small, but they can survive because of the depth of the lake and the springs feeding it. They have a jellyfish day every year and lots of people come to check them out."

"That is always fun," Elisabeth said.

"This lake seems like a smaller version of the lake Pontius Pilate retired to after the whole Jerusalem fiasco. The lore is the lake would turn blood red each Good Friday because of the shrimp colonies. It was for him to wash off the blood that was on his hands. They say he was given that

270

purgatory to help him find solace for his deeds unto humanity," Edward said.

"Oh, really?" Trinity asked. "I never knew that one."

"Well, it might have some truth to it, but it's a good story," Edward replied.

"It is getting late now and this has been a long day, let alone a long next few days, so I think we should all turn in to rest up," Trinity said.

"That's a good idea," Tom replied, and they all went to their rooms to get some sleep.

The night was still and very quiet. The light from the stars filled up the sky. The cool night air was perfect for sleeping and they all rested well throughout the night.

The next day, the paper came to the front door. It was the regional news and Tom picked it up to have something to read during breakfast. Trinity was in the kitchen making coffee and Edward was setting up the cable box on the television to get some morning news.

"Ok, there you go," Edward said. "All set up and logged in. Good thing there is still a connection to the world way out here."

Tom turned the page and set the paper down. "Trinity?" he asked stoically.

"What?" she asked.

"Right there," Tom said as he pointed to the paper.

Trinity walked over to the table and leaned down to see. "Oh my, this is going to be wild now. Edward, there is an article in the regional news about the diamond beanie bear," she said.

"You have got to be kidding me! Already?"

"They must have picked it up off the wire from the local news," Trinity said.

"So, now what?" Edward asked.

"I am not sure, but when Elisabeth gets in here for breakfast, we need to have her call her friend Melody," Trinity said.

"Yes, that is a good idea," Tom said.

"Oh, there you are," Trinity said. "We were just talking about you."

"What now?" Elisabeth asked as she rolled her eyes.

"It's in the regional news now!" Trinity said.

"Oh, no. I need to call Melody."

"Yes, you do," Trinity said.

Elisabeth went to get her phone off the charger and dialed Melody. Melody picked up in short order.

"Hello, this is Elisabeth."

"Yes, oh, wow, I needed to talk to you. Where are you?"

"I am at a friend's cottage, hiding out."

"Oh, good. I am at a friend of my mom's. I am hiding out too. You know it is really crazy right now."

"Yes, I'm sorry. I should have warned you that if this ever got out, it would get crazy."

"It's crazy, but kind of neat too. What do you think we should do now?"

"I am not sure. My mom, dad, and our friend from England are here and we are deciding what to do. I will call you to tell you our plan as soon as we know."

"Alright, but I don't think I can wait too long. I need to get back to work, but only after this settles down. You see, I was called in to the administrator's office before I came over here. He told me the hospital was almost unmanageable because of all the people coming around asking about the diamond bear. I told him I was sorry, but it wasn't anything we could control. He understood and told me I was a great employee, so he would give me paid time off until this quieted down. I told him we need to secure the diamond bear for now and he said he already had. He said he placed the bear in the office safe behind the picture. He said only very few people knew the safe was there, but only he and I would know the combination. He helped me get out of the hospital without being seen before I came here."

"Good, I am glad you are safe. We will get this figured out, don't worry. I will call you as soon as I know the plan."

"Ok, thanks. I will be waiting to hear from you."

"Alright, bye for now," Elisabeth said, as she ended the call.

"There you go," Elisabeth said. "Melody is safe for now, but we have to get this figured out. Every national media outlet is going to be looking for us. When we tell them there is more than one diamond bear, let alone two hundred bears, this will erupt like a volcano. It will spread worldwide in days. Every beanie bear will become sought after like it was the mid-nineties all over again times a thousand."

"You are right," Tom said, as he looked at Trinity. "If only your wily mom was here to tell us what to do. She set this whole thing up, so I hope she has a plan to keep it under control. She must have known how it would play out."

"That is such a nice thing to say about my mom, dear," Trinity said. "You are right, she set it up for us, but I guess we have to figure it out."

"Then we need to be ready to be here a while. I am going to unpack my suitcase, and put my things into the dresser," Edward said, and he got up and went to his room.

Chapter 30 Suitcase

Edward took the old suitcase he got from Ida's house and placed it on the bed to unpack. He took everything out and neatly put it into the dresser. He checked the other pockets of the suitcase to make sure he didn't miss anything in the bottoms. Trinity was walking down the hallway near his room and peered in.

"Everything ok there, Edward?" she asked. "I am sorry you are mixed up in this. I know you don't want to be stuck here when you could be out sightseeing."

"Oh, it's ok, Trinity. It's kind of fun. Besides, I have time yet."

Trinity looked at the suitcase he had and her eyes lit up. "Where did you get that suitcase from?" she asked.

"Oh, this old thing? I found it in the back of the closet at your mom's house. I hope you don't mind, but it was a lot bigger than mine. I needed extra room for more things in case we were going to be out here for a while."

"I don't mind, but I haven't seen that since I was a teenager. You know, that is a trick suitcase."

"A what?"

"A trick suitcase. You see, it has a hidden compartment in the bottom. I always thought it was really cool because I had never seen anything like it."

"Oh, yeah? Where is the compartment?"

"It's right here. You raise this up and push the hidden latch and then it opens."

"Oh, I see now," he said as he pushed the latch and opened the lid. It sprung open like something was pressing against it. He looked and saw that there was something there. It was a book that looked like a journal of sorts. It had a flowery pattern on the cover. They were both beside themselves at the discovery. Trinity carefully picked it up and looked at it.

"What is it?" Edward asked.

"I can't believe it! It's my mom's old diary! She used to keep notes in it."

"That is too cool," Edward said.

"Yes, but this is strange. I had wondered what happened to this. Let's take it into the living room to show the others and see what's in it."

"Yes, let's go," Edward replied.

They went into the living room and called Tom and Elisabeth over.

"Hey, look what popped out of your grandma's old suitcase that Edward brought," Trinity said.

"What is it?" Elisabeth asked.

"It is my mom's old diary," Trinity said.

"Oh, cool! What does it say?" Elisabeth asked.

"I don't know. I never looked at it," Trinity said.

"You never looked at it?" Tom asked.

"No, not ever," Trinity replied.

"Well, there's no better time than the present," Tom said.

"Yeah, Mom, what's in it?" Elisabeth said.

"Ok, ok, I will look and see," Trinity said.

As Trinity turned the cover of the diary, it seemed to gracefully open on its own. Each page drifted from right to left in unison and they fluttered as if they were under some magical spell. Trinity leafed through to see if there was any order to it so she could decide where to start.

Trinity saw that one page was creased in the corner, so she turned to it. The page had some instructions on it that began with the words "Beanie Bears" written at the top.

"Hmm," Trinity said.

She read for a few seconds until everyone else exclaimed at once, "What is it?"

"Oh, ok," Trinity said as she came out of her silent reading. "It says here that Ida had set up a treasure hunt of sorts and it enumerates her desires. She says she hopes this diary finds us well and that the beanie bears are a fun adventure she

280

hopes we truly enjoy. She knows it will be trying at times, but we are to please take everything in stride and enjoy the adventure we are already in. She asks that we be very judicious with the bears. We should only keep three bears each for our own and auction off ten bears. We are to use the Christie's auction house for a charity, or charities if the proceeds are large enough. She tells us to take the others and send them out to other anonymous places for others to find, as this was her greatest joy over the years to leave these special bears at places people would never expect. She said she went to church bazaars, she sent some to online auctions, and left some at poor houses. She placed some on benches anonymously so a needy child could find it. She would find any way to send them out to the farthest reaches she could. She would send some in boxes of clothes to distant Salvation Army stores and even put some in care packages for the Red Cross during world disasters. She says to be as creative as we can and to have the bears make it out to everyone in the fairest possible way. She wants us to release the bears in any way we see fit, but we are to try and take our time so that they come in to the market slowly over a span of time. The initial rush will invariably quiet down. The bears we have will need to be let out to give others a chance to have one in time. Her plan was to keep her patience by slowly releasing the bears and she would like it to continue."

"Oh, my, that is wild," Edward said. "She was quite the planner, wasn't she?"

"Yes, that's my grandma," Elisabeth said.

"You got that right," Tom replied.

"Wait, there is more," Trinity said. "The diary says the same person who administered the messages in the bottles has the ability to authenticate each of the bears. The documentation he has is protected from everyone. The documentation he has will never be released and those who find the bears can send them to him to verify their authenticity for free. His firm will send the bear back with all expenses paid, along with a certificate of authenticity. He will also inventory the bears that are submitted. The bears that are sent in and proven to be forgeries will be sent back at the sender's expense."

"Wow, that is so cool," Elisabeth said.

"She sure has this all worked out, doesn't she?" Trinity said. "We need to call Matthew and see what he has, now that we know he is involved. I think I still have his number in my phone. Good thing I haven't upgraded this phone yet." Trinity flashed a big smile at Elisabeth, who had been trying to get her to upgrade to a newer, faster phone, so she could be hip and cool again.

"Yeah, Mom, you got me there," Elisabeth said.

"Here it is, right here. I knew I still had his phone number," Trinity said. She pressed the send button to dial Matthew's number. "It should be about late afternoon there, right now." She lifted the phone to her ear and it rang a few times before Matthew answered.

"Hello?" Matthew said, in his British accent.

"Yes, hello, my name is Trinity. I don't know if you remember me, but I was calling to find out about some information you might have."

"Trinity who?" he responded.

"I am Trinity, the daughter of the lady who set up the message in a bottle treasure hunt. I was one of the judges that verified the authenticity of each finder."

"Oh, yes!" he interrupted. "It was your mom's plan and your daughter came along too."

"Yes, you remember us, then?"

"Yes, I do. Let me bring up the file. You didn't find another bottle, did you?"

"No, but that would be fun, wouldn't it?"

"Yes, it would. I haven't had any more come through, but quite honestly I was hoping to see some more. The more time that passes by, the less chance there is that one will be found. Oh, here they are, the documents with the instructions. What were you looking for? I will check the documents over to see if I can release the information you may need."

"I am looking for any information you might have about beanie bears."

"Bean what?" Matthew exclaimed. "Did I hear you right? Beanie bears? You mean the beanie babies from the nineties?"

"Yes, those are the ones," Trinity confirmed.

"Why would I have information about those? Am I missing something here?"

"No, you aren't. This may sound out of place, but my mom wrote in a diary that you have information about the beanie bears."

"Is this an April Fool's prank call?"

"No, it's not," Trinity laughed. "I would think we were off center too if I wasn't involved this far myself. No, my mom has some beanie bear adventure going on. She said you would have the information about it and would be able to verify the authenticity of each bear. You were given funds to pay for it all."

"Well, I am sorry, but I have just scrolled through all the documents and there is nothing here about beanie bears, I can assure you. Wait a second, I see a scanned page with a corner folded over. There appears to be some writing on the back. Let me check the vault and pull out the original documents to see. Can I call you back at this number?"

"Yes, please do. We will be here."

"Alright, I will talk to you soon," Matthew said.

"Thank you. We will be waiting, but not patiently. Bye, bye," Trinity said.

Chapter 31 Matthew

Matthew phoned down to the vault level and requested the documents to be sent up to him. He gave them the file number and was on the edge of his seat waiting. While he was waiting, he went back through the other file to see if there was something he had missed before. There had to be a clue somewhere to tip him off or maybe this was just a wild goose chase. He was not really willing to believe that though, because the past events all turned out to be true.

He heard a knock on his door frame. He turned to see a young man standing in the open doorway with a manila packet.

"Is this what you were looking for, sir?" the young man asked, in a very thick British accent.

"Yes, yes, that was fast," Matthew said.

"Well, we pride ourselves on being organized down on the vault level. We respond as quickly as we can, but really the answer is that we all know what's in this file. We have always been interested in this story. The daily folklore around here is that everyone wants to find one of those bottles. One of those bottles is better than a pint of Westvleteren!" the young man said.

"Yes, I feel the same. Thanks for getting this so quickly."

Matthew grabbed the file and cleared his desk. He opened up the manila envelope and immediately turned it over to the back. There was a bunch of typing. He remembered vaguely seeing that typing before, but at the time he thought it was just some old recycled paper that Ida was using because she had run out. There before his eyes was a list of beanie bears detailed with each of their unique identifiers. Each bear had multiple identification items. There was a note on the bottom.

This list is for your eyes only and can never be divulged. It is to remain proprietary. This list identifies each bear. It will give you the ability to authenticate each one for the finder or the owner. The account number herein contains an amount of money more than sufficient enough to pay for your services. The items for account retrieval are provided here and also verified in the message account. Please take care of the list and keep the adventure alive. I trust this finds you well.

"Oh that Ida," Matthew thought. "She was a really neat lady." Matthew set the file down to pick up the phone to dial Trinity.

"Hello," Trinity said.

"Hello, again, this is Matthew. I don't know how to tell you this and I cannot believe it much myself. Your mom did leave those beanie bears and she did leave funds for verification. I also found a list for verification of each bear, but that is all I can tell you. I can't release the identifiers, but there are others only shown in this list."

"Oh, thank you, I was hoping you had good news. We are at our wits' end here and this is about to go out of control, so we really needed to hear this. We are so happy the notes in her diary are true and found you well."

"Yes, I have it all here, so send them my way and I will take care of it per these instructions."

"Thanks so much, Matthew. We will be in touch, then," Trinity said.

"Thank you for all your help, too, and Godspeed," Matthew replied.

Trinity ended the call and looked over at everyone else. "Ok, then it is official. This is on. Matthew has the verification instructions just like the diary said and he can take care of all of it. We need to figure out how we want to handle this now."

"Well, we could go to the newspaper and do an article on it," Tom said.

"I don't think Mom wanted that. We need to do what she wanted and go on a national morning show," Trinity said.

"I am not sure I am ready for that," Tom replied.

"Me, neither," Elisabeth said.

"Oh, it will be fun," Edward said. "We can do this and do this together."

"Well, you may be right," Elisabeth said. "Maybe we could do this together. I guess it would be fun."

"Alright, I see your point," Tom said. "So how do we do this?"

"I am not sure. You can't just dial a major network and get on the morning show, like snapping your fingers," Trinity said.

Just then Elisabeth's phone notification went off again. "Well, I guess maybe you can," Trinity said laughing. Elisabeth swiped her phone and saw it was another update from Melody's social page.

"It seems Melody can!" Elisabeth quipped. "She has some messages from some major network producers trying to get a hold of her. I will text her and tell her to call me." Elisabeth texted Melody and she called Elisabeth right back.

"Oh, my gosh!" Melody exclaimed. "I can't take any more of this! I have all the major television and news channels hounding me. I don't want to go on television! I could never do it."

"That's what I wanted to talk to you about. We have some information that could put all of this in context. We need to get one of those contacts from you so we can get on television to get this all out there and under control," Elisabeth said.

"Which one do you want?"

"I don't know. Let me ask my family." Elisabeth repeated what Melody told her. "Which television show do we want?" Elisabeth asked.

"How about the one I always watch in the morning?" Trinity said.

"Yeah, what is that one called? *Good Morning Friends*?" Tom asked.

"Yes, that one," Trinity said.

"Really, Mom? That one is huge. They will not get us on for weeks," Elisabeth said.

"Maybe so, but we should try anyway. It will get us the most exposure," Trinity said.

"You are right about that," Tom said.

"Then ask her for the *Good Morning Friends* show producer, Elisabeth," Trinity said.

Elisabeth asked Melody if she had a contact for them, so she looked through her messages.

"Yes, here it is!" Melody said excitedly. "I will forward it to your phone. Please take care of this. I need to get back to work and some normalcy."

"Ok, we will," Elisabeth replied. "See you soon or maybe you will see us first on television."

"I hope so," Melody said.

Elisabeth ended the call and waited for the notification of a new text. "Beep, beep," the phone went.

"There it is," Edward said.

"What does it say?" Trinity asked hurriedly.

"Please call this producer as soon as possible," Elisabeth said.

"Hurry up and call them!" Edward said.

"Ok, ok, I will do it. Just give me a moment to get ready for this ride," Elisabeth said.

She pressed the number in the text message to dial the contact. It rang twice until somebody answered.

"Good morning friends, how may I help you?"

Elisabeth was speechless. She tried to talk but nothing came out.

"Well, answer them, dear," Tom said.

"Uh, hello, this is Elisabeth. I am calling to speak with the producer of the *Good Morning Friends* show."

"I'm sorry, but everyone is really busy right now. Can I ask what you are calling about?"

"Yes, we are calling about the diamond beanie bear."

Just as Elisabeth finished the word bear, the operator said, "Will you hold please? If you get disconnected, call right back and ask for Juday."

"Ok, thank you."

"Hold please," the operator repeated.

Elisabeth could hear the phone clicking several times. She held her breath and waited for someone to pick up on the other end.

Chapter 32 Juday

The phone clicked two more times and a lady answered.

"Hello?" a booming, female voice said. "How may I help you?"

"Hello, my name is Elisabeth and I am calling about the diamond beanie bear situation. You see, my mom, my dad, and our friend, Edward, are in possession of the diamond beanie bears. We want to know if you would like us to come on your show to discuss the situation surrounding the bears."

"You are the ones with the diamond bears?"

"Yes, we have some of the bears in our possession and would like to shed some light on them."

"You have the diamond bears with you right now?"

"Yes, we have several of them," Elisabeth said.

"There is more than one?" Juday interrupted.

"Why, yes, there are two hundred of them."

"Can I put you on speaker phone?" Juday asked.

"Yes, why?" The phone clicked and Elisabeth could hear a change in tone.

"You are on speaker phone with our production staff. Could you tell us how many diamond bears there are and how you know this?" Juday asked.

"There are two hundred of them and we know this because my grandmother, Ida, set it all up. We have verified the truth about the bears and we have multiple forms of verification evidence to prove it."

"What can you provide for us now to prove, at least in part, the truth to your story?"

"Yes, what do you have that we could look up right now?" another person in the room with Juday asked.

"Well, I am not sure," Elisabeth said. "What do we have to prove our story?" she asked everyone around her.

"What are they asking for?" Trinity replied.

"They are asking for some verification of the diamond bears, because they want to be sure we are telling the truth," Elisabeth said.

"Yes," Juday said. "We have had a lot of calls about this, as you can imagine. They have all been loose ends. Everyone is jumping on this story, but none of them told us there was more than one bear."

"Oh, I see," Elisabeth replied. "Well, let us see what we could give you to prove this."

Edward, Trinity, and Tom looked at each other quizzically.

"What do we know?" Tom asked.

"We know the lists," Edward replied.

"Yes, the lists. You got them from public records," Tom said.

"Yes, we did," Trinity said. "The one list is from the County Recorder's Office. I have the receipt right here."

"What will that prove?" Elisabeth asked.

"It proves they could see it for themselves," Trinity said.

"That would work, but they have to go to the County Recorder to check on it," Edward said. Edward started to look through the pile of documents on the table. "Oh, wait, here is the receipt from the Recorder and on the bottom is the website where they could look up the deed online."

"Yes, that will do," Elisabeth said. She turned back to the phone. "Ok, we have something. There is a list in our local Recorder's Office. They also have a web portal to look at things online." Elisabeth gave Juday the web address and the document number.

"Hold on for a minute," Juday said. "George, would you look this up quickly?" Juday asked. "We need to verify this right now and I

300

don't want to lose this phone connection with them."

George typed the website address, brought up the webpage, and entered the document number. "Alright, I have it up, but it doesn't look like a list."

"You have to zoom in with the browser to see the list," Elisabeth said. She thought to herself, "I hope it shows up because the print is blurry, but maybe the scan is more detailed."

"Hold on, I think I see something in the border," George said.

"What is it?" Juday asked.

"It is a list of some sort and it looks like it says beanie bears."

"How many are there?" Juday asked.

"Well, the largest number on here is two hundred," George said.

"Alright, Elisabeth, you have my attention," Juday said. "Now what?"

"I don't know," Elisabeth said. "We were thinking that we want to get on the morning show to give an interview about what we know so we can see where it leads."

"This is what I can do," Juday said. "Can you get to an airport in about two hours?"

Elisabeth is stunned and turned to everyone else. "They are asking if we can get to an airport in the next two hours."

"What?" Tom exclaimed. "We are going to be on the show?"

"They want us now?" Trinity asked.

"Yes, it sounds like it," Elisabeth replied.

"Well, what are you waiting for? Tell them yes!" Edward said.

"Yes, we can do that," Elisabeth told Juday.

"Good! Which airport will you be flying out from?" Juday asked.

"Uh, how about South Bend, I guess," Elisabeth replied.

"We will get that taken care of. You just need to show up and check in with the airline. You only need to show them your identification and they will have everything ready for you," Juday said. "You will need to text me the names of everyone in your party, so we can secure your tickets. We will take care of it on our end."

"Should I text you at this number?" Elisabeth asked.

"No, I will send you my personal cell number," Juday said.

"Ok, I will text you on that one. Thanks for everything," Elisabeth said.

"No, I thank you for calling us. It is our pleasure to break this scoop. We will have you flown in for tomorrow's show," Juday said.

"Tomorrow's show? Really?" Elisabeth said shockingly.

"Yes, so we need to get you here early to run through the scenario."

"That would be good, because we have a lot to tell you," Elisabeth said.

"We will see you tomorrow. Don't worry. We will take care of everything for you," Juday said.

"Thank you, Juday. We will see you tomorrow, bright and early."

"Goodbye, and travel safe," Juday said.

Elisabeth, still dazed, ended the conversation with Juday. Trinity looked over at Tom and said, "Could you please call your friend, the deputy, and see if he could go over and watch the house? If we are going to be on the morning show, there will certainly be a lot of people around our house knowing we were on the show."

"Yes, that is a good idea. I will call him. He should have a few days off his swing shift, so maybe he could stay at the house to watch over it. He could leave his marked car in the driveway."

"That would be nice and it would help out our neighbor if things get heated over there," Trinity said.

"That's a good thought," Tom replied. He called his friend and sure enough, he was off for three days and was happy to help. He had a key for the house and he agreed to go over there later in the evening after he stopped at his own home.

Chapter 33 Roundabout

They all packed their bags light for a quick, overnight stay. They piled into Trinity's car and Tom drove. They headed east, on the old state road, to the local regional airport. The road wound through a small, sleepy community of very quaint and impeccably kept homes. There wasn't much to see, and there weren't any large stores or restaurants, but it was very nice and quiet. It was a great place to visit on a weekend getaway trip to enjoy the peace and quiet and to rest and reenergize.

The old state road took some quick winding curves on the east side of town and the horizon opened up to reveal some vast farms fields. They drove down the state road and admired its gentle curves through the fields. They could see, out in the distance, some large factories that seemed out of place, but they were productive nonetheless.

The drive was short and it was only a little while until they could see a burgeoning city on the horizon, with a respectable sized airport on the west side. They drove past the southern edge near the runways, to a small parking lot, after they travelled through a newer roundabout.

Trinity was happy Tom was driving, as each time she had to go there she never felt comfortable maneuvering through the roundabout. She never understood the need to tear up all the land and homes to put it in. It did help traffic move in a more constant pattern, but it did it at the cost of pedestrian traffic and a whole bunch of ground, including turning an old neighborhood completely inside out. She had always wondered about the need to utilize a roundabout and if it was worth it.

The parking lot was easily accessible and the parking rates were very cheap compared to parking at the airport in Chicago.

"This is what I like about it," Tom said. "Look at those rates. We really save money here, not only because it's closer, but because when we get back, we don't have to take out a car loan to get our car out of the parking lot."

"Yeah, yeah, Dad," Elisabeth replied. "We hear that every time we come here," she said smiling.

"Yes, I know, but the extra airfare cost is worth it to me. I really don't like going to Chicago because your mom always makes me drive and then she gets so tense when we get on the expressways. I know she never says anything, but I can see she has a death grip on the armrest the whole time." Trinity looked over and smiled at Tom.

"Yeah, Dad, you are right," Elisabeth said. "We need to park and get in to the airport to check in."

"Check in? This ought to be a treat. We have no known reservations or known seats. We are flying blind here," Tom said.

"But it sure is fun!" Edward replied.

They parked and grabbed their bags out of the trunk and made their way into the terminal. The terminal was very nice, but quite empty and quiet. It was not like other major airports, with the hustle and bustle of people moving about everywhere. They walked right up to the ticket agent, who seemed to be bored, but happy to see customers.

"Hello, how are you today?" she said.

"Oh, we are fine," Tom replied. "We are not sure how to proceed, but we need to be on a flight to LaGuardia later tonight, to be in New York tomorrow morning."

"Hmm, that sounds out of place. Let's see about the flight that is just about to leave here. It is the last flight out to LaGuardia, so I can check to make sure it lands before eleven o'clock east coast time. The airport has a curfew for planes, so if you are not on this last flight, you will have to wait until tomorrow."

"Oh, so we need to be on that flight," Tom said.

"Do you have your reservations?" the agent asked.

"I am not sure, we were only told to bring our identification to check in," Tom said.

"Let me see your identification and I will see if you have reservations."

Tom handed her his identification and she leaned it against her monitor and typed in his name. The computer beeped and the screen changed. The screen facing them also changed to display "LaGuardia" with a departure time.

"There it is," Edward said. "That's the flight."

"Yes, I have it right here. You are on this flight and you have been upgraded to first class," the agent said.

"First class?" Tom said and smiled widely. "That is great! I could use some relaxation after the adventures we've had the last few days!"

Trinity kicked Tom in the shin and his head spun toward her. "Enough. Be quiet," she mouthed to him, but Tom dismissed her with a wily smile.

"You are checked in. Can I see everyone else's identification?" the agent asked.

The all extended their hands out to give the agent their identification at the same time. They were all very excited to have first class coming their way.

"Alright, then, you are all ready to go now. Head through security if all you have are checked bags," the agent said.

They thanked the agent and made their way toward security. The security gate was the typical, over reaching, intrusive type, but it didn't take long for the passengers to go through it. The agents seemed somewhat welcoming during a normally quiet time. They picked up all their things from the scanner and only had to walk a short distance to the waiting area. They easily found seats to sit in until the plane was ready to embark.

Elisabeth heard her phone ring in her pocket and reached in to check it.

"Hello?" Elisabeth said.

"Hello, how are you doing?" a lady asked.

"We are fine. Is this Juday?"

"Yes, it is. I was calling to make sure you were en route and everything was good."

"Oh, yes, everything is very good. I see we are in first class, so we thank you."

312

"You're welcome," Juday said. "I was also calling to see if you could send us a picture of each one of you and some clothing sizes. If you need some apparel to wear on the show, we can have some different outfits ready for you to choose from when you get to the studio."

"Oh, that would be nice! We could do that."

"When you get them to me, I will take care of the rest. Oh, wait, you need to know that when you get here, after you leave the gate area, there will be a driver waiting for you. He will be in the pick-up area right outside of the security exit gate. He will be holding a sign that says "Diamond" on it. Make sure to only talk to that driver and no one else. He will not come up to you. Anyone else that approaches you is not your guy. He will be holding the sign and wearing a *Good Morning Friends* jacket."

"Alright, we will look for him."

"Have a pleasant trip. We are all anxiously waiting for you to get you here tomorrow. It's going to be a great show."

"Oh, we can hardly wait! See you tomorrow. Bye, bye."

Elisabeth pushed the end button on her phone and told the others what Juday said. As she was telling them about the driver, Trinity's phone rang. She grabbed it and looked at the number. It was their neighbor, so she answered.

"Hello, how are you doing?" Trinity asked.

"Hello, I am doing ok, but how are things going for you?" her neighbor replied.

"Well, I was hoping you would call. Tom asked his deputy friend to come over and watch the house on his days off because we are going to New York. We are going to be on a morning television show. I can explain when we get back. You don't need to worry about the house."

"Oh, good, because I was getting worried. There is an unusual amount of traffic on our county road. It's normally quiet, so I was wondering what was going on. That's why I had to call you."

"I was hoping you wouldn't get too worried, but you say there are a lot of people driving around?"

"Yes, there are a lot of people. It's like downtown around here and people are slowing down right in front of your house."

"Hmm, well it's good we have a deputy staying there. He should have his marked car parked in front of the house."

"Yes, there is a marked car in your driveway. I was wondering about that. Between the police car and the traffic, I knew something was up."

"You are right, something is up. We are on our way to the *Good Morning Friends* show that will be on tomorrow morning."

"What? You are kidding me! I was just watching the end of the evening sitcoms and there was this big promotional commercial for the *Good Morning Friends* show. There is a big reveal happening tomorrow and we are supposed to tune in to find out about the people behind the big secret of the diamond beanie bears."

Trinity is stunned and she could feel her face turn cold.

"You heard what?" Trinity asked.

"Yeah, it was on just a few minutes ago. I remember it vividly. I swear it was just on. Hey, wait, there it is on again, a big reveal tomorrow about the diamond beanie bears. It says to be sure to watch tomorrow. Is that about you?"

"Um," Trinity stammered. "Yes, it is us," she finally said. "We are the ones behind the diamond bears. I can tell you all about it when we get back, but for now, please watch over the house. Can you help Tom's friend when he needs it? Tomorrow will be even wackier after the show is on."

"Oh, you said a mouthful there," Tom replied in the background.

"I will watch the house, but you have to promise to tell me all about it," the neighbor said.

"I will, and thanks. I owe you a lot," Trinity said.

"You're welcome. Have a safe trip and a fun show."

"We will. Bye, bye," Trinity said.

Trinity ended the call and told all of them what was happening with the traffic around the house and the promotional commercials about the show. Tom looked stunned and could not believe it.

"I think this is great! This is going to be so fun!" Elisabeth said.

"Yes, this will be," Edward said.

"I don't know about fun, but it sure will be interesting," Tom said, and he settled back in his chair to wait for the flight.

Chapter 34 First Class

Edward got up and went over to the check in podium. He asked the agent if she could change the channel on the television monitor to the network that ran the *Good Morning Friends* show.

"Oh, sure I can. Let me see what channel that is on," she said.

She flipped through the channels until she found the right one. The show was going into a commercial break, but it only showed the commercials from the typical Fortune 500 companies trying to sell their branded products. Then just before the sitcom came back on, the network ran the promotional spot for the upcoming shows. They played the one for the morning show and it was just like the neighbor said.

"Tune in tomorrow to the *Good Morning Friends* show, where the guests will reveal the mystery sweeping the nation surrounding the instant sensation of the diamond beanie bears. Stay tuned to hear more and find out tomorrow about this exclusive story," the commercial said.

They all just stood there, stunned and speechless. They knew they could not say anything, not even the most remote words, or else they would tip their hand as to who they were and where they were going.

The plane was ready and since they were first class passengers, they boarded first, but it really didn't matter much because the number of passengers was small. They all got onto the plane and to their large, comfortable, first class seats.

Tom relaxed deeply into his cushy chair and let out a big sigh. He felt like he could doze off very quickly in that chair. He stretched out his legs, fastened his seatbelt, and laid back to close his eyes. He had heard the emergency routine so many times he could recite it in his sleep. He grinned and tried to doze off for a bit before they took off.

Everyone was extremely content in their seats and the plane seemed to leave quickly. The pilot came on over the intercom and thanked them for flying that evening.

"The trip will be a little quicker since we have to make it to LaGuardia before the flight curfew tonight, but we have clear skies and things should go smoothly," the pilot said.

The flight was very nice and Tom caught up on some very relaxing sleep. He even missed the fantastic food that was only served to the first class passengers. The plane started on the descent. Tom instinctively woke up as his body told him they would be landing shortly. The plane came in over a dark body of water. In an instant a runway appeared, seemingly out of nowhere, just in time to catch the plane falling out of the sky.

The pilot adeptly rolled onto the runway and applied the speedbrakes to slow the plane down quickly on a shorter runway. The plane slowed and then taxied to the gate. They got to disembark first as they were in first class and they passed the baggage collection area and security.

As soon as they went past the posted guards, they saw a man with a sign, just like Juday described. They approached him and he was looking at his phone intently, but as they neared, he looked up.

"I am here to give you a lift to your hotel. You do look just like your pictures. Did you just take them a little while ago, because the clothes you are wearing now are the same clothes in your pictures?" the driver asked.

They all smiled and replied, "Yes, it's us."

"If you have everything you need, I am right outside the door here. I have someone in the car waiting to go. You know these new security rules. We can't leave our car unless someone is in it."

"Yes, it's not like it used to be," Tom said.

They walked out through the automatic doors and there was a perfectly clean, brand new limousine. At least it looked new, or else it was perfectly kept. The concierge opened the door for them and they all piled in. It was extremely nice and perfectly appointed.

"Now, Tom, don't get too comfortable. This is only a short ride," Trinity said.

"Yes, I know, but it wouldn't take much for me to get comfortable in this," he said smiling.

They watched the city lights pass by the windows. As they crossed the old, picturesque bridge to Manhattan, they could see the city skyline all lit up in the night. It was a sight to see and they all peered out the windows to watch it get closer and closer until they were right in it.

The streets were busy and the traffic was everywhere. The buildings towered over them on every side and it seemed like the energy from the city seeped into their car. It was a sense of being alive and vibrant. The driver adeptly maneuvered through the traffic and soon they were stopped in front of an old building. It was of normal size compared to the others, and it seemed that it was a quiet hotel. Elisabeth looked out the window and read the sign over the porte cochere.

"Hey look, it's Gramercy Park Hotel," Elisabeth said.

"Oh, how nice," Trinity said. "This is such a hidden gem in the middle of the metropolis."

"Yes, this is a really nice place," Tom said. "I have heard this is the place to be in town. I heard that sometimes a lot of celebrities stay here to keep out of the limelight. This will be perfect for us after tomorrow."

"Yes, you are right. This will work out well," Edward said.

They got out of the limousine and walked into the old, well remodeled hotel lobby. It was filled with artistic furnishings and had the aura of old architectural elegance throughout. They walked up to the front desk to check in and the clerk had keys for each room in no time. The concierge helped them to their rooms and wouldn't take a tip. He said it was all taken care of and very well indeed. The rooms were completely charming and they all settled in to get some much needed rest. The city seemed hushed while they were in their rooms and it was a very pleasant night's sleep.

The morning broke as the sunshine crept into their rooms through the crack of the curtains. Even though it was too early to get up, none of them could sleep well anyway knowing what the morning would bring. Elisabeth was getting ready when her phone rang. It was on the charger cord as she picked it up.

"Hello?" she said.

"Hello, we are ready to go downstairs and get a bite to eat before we leave," Trinity said.

"Oh, ok, I will meet you down there in a minute."

"We will save you a seat and some orange juice."

"Thanks," Elisabeth said. She finished getting ready and headed to the elevator to go to the dining room for some breakfast. As she was walking down the hall, Edward came out of his room and nearly ran into her.

"Oh, hey, I was heading downstairs to get some breakfast," he said.

"Me, too. My mom and dad are down there saving a seat for us. I am starving."

"Yeah, all this excitement uses up a lot of energy."

They rode the elevator down to the dining level and walked into the lush, extravagantly furnished dining room. It was calm and quiet except for the sound of fine china ringing once in a while.

"There they are," Edward said. "They're over there."

They were seated next to the large bay window. There were fresh flowers in large vases in the window sill. The sun was beaming through the stained glass panes and it created a soothing setting to eat breakfast in. They sat down in the chairs and the waiter came to serve them immediately. Breakfast was truly delightful and the food was fantastic. Elisabeth was sitting back in her chair when her phone started ringing. It broke the calm silence of the room, so she answered it as quickly as she could.

"Hello," Juday said.

"Hi Juday, we were just eating breakfast."

"That's good, because it will be a long day, so make sure you get enough to eat. The food there is spectacular."

"You are right, it is quite wonderful."

"You will have a driver waiting out front for you, so all you need to do is jump in, and he will get you to the studio lickity split. Don't worry

326

about your rooms or your bags. We have that all taken care of. When you get here, my assistant will direct you to a stage room to see if you would like to choose an outfit we have for you up here. I will be in as soon as I can get a free moment."

"Alright, we will see you in a little while then," Elisabeth replied.

"See you in a bit," Juday said.

Elisabeth told them Juday had it all set up and the driver was waiting out front for them. They asked the waiter for the check and he said it was all taken care, including the tip. He thanked them for coming and told them to come back again. They grabbed their things and went to the front lobby to find the receptionist going over schedules. Before they could ask, the driver got up from his large, high back chair and introduced himself. He said the car was right out front and if they were ready, he could get them going. They all shook their heads that they were ready and they climbed into the car.

Chapter 35 Stars

Edward was sitting in the front with the driver where he could watch all the traffic surrounding them.

"This is a smaller sedan than yesterday," Edward said.

"Yes, it is. The large limousine is a bear to maneuver through traffic during the day, so we always use the sedan to make it through the streets quicker," the driver said.

Edward could see how the traffic moved along the streets in an orchestrated pattern. The lines marked on the pavement seemed to mean nothing to the drivers, and the traffic flowed seamlessly down each street. If a car was pulling over to the side to drop someone off or pick someone up, the rest of the traffic didn't flinch a bit. It flowed right around the stopped car like a stream of water flowing effortlessly through its channel.

The ride went very smooth. Edward could not believe how all the cars worked together to get to their destinations.

"Here we are," the driver said. He pulled over to a small curb cut out along the street in front of a large building.

"Oh, I see," Tom said. "It's the studio we usually see on television."

"Yes, this is the same one," Trinity said.

"This is so neat," Elisabeth said.

"You just need to go in the front door. I will make sure to beep them to tell them you just walked into the lobby. Someone will be right there to help you," the driver said.

They all got out of the car and went into the building. Just like the driver said, Juday's assistant was there to help them find their way up to the studio.

"I hope everything is going well," the assistant said.

"Oh, yes, it's all very nice," Trinity replied. "Thank you."

"We are going up to the second floor to get you to the setup room. If there is anything you

330

need, please push the intercom call button, and someone will be right there."

The assistant walked them up a flight of stairs and down a hall to an open door. It opened into a large room. Inside were a couple of makeup desks and a large, open closet filled with brand new outfits on store hangers.

"Hey, look here," Elisabeth said. "These must be our choices for outfits to wear."

"These are wonderful," Trinity said, as she pushed the hangers across the bar to look at each outfit. "Oh, I think this one is just right."

"Ooh, I like this one," Elisabeth said.

Edward and Tom were standing to the side and were busy looking out the open door. They were trying to see who would walk by and who would be on the show that morning as guests.

"Oh, here dear, this one is good for you," Trinity said. She took an outfit off the bar and gave it to Tom. He didn't even look at it. He simply took it from her and agreed that it would be fine.

331

Edward turned to look at the choices, found one he really liked, and took it off the rack. Elisabeth had already made it into the changing room and came out quickly.

"This one is really nice. It's a designer original. This looks like it was tailored just for me," she said excitedly.

"It looks fantastic on you," Trinity replied.

Tom was in the changing room and came out to show Trinity his outfit.

"Oh, that is nice, dear," Trinity said.

"Yes, and it fits so well too," he said.

Trinity took her turn next and put on the outfit she chose. "It fits perfectly," she said. She turned around several times to check herself in the mirror.

"Now that looks really nice," Tom said.

Edward changed into his outfit and was ready in a flash. They all sat in the plush chairs in the room and looked to see if there were any treats for them to snack on. A tall, refined older woman walked in.

"Hello there, it's nice to meet you in person. I'm Juday. It looks like the outfits worked out well. You all look great in them. We will need to get the makeup crew in here to get you completely ready for the cameras. I will inform the crew of the colors of your outfits, so they can adjust the cameras and lighting. We will make you look like a million bucks for our viewing audience. This is a big day. I am so happy you chose to be on our show. We are all extremely excited to have you here. If this goes as well as I think it will, it will be an award winning show today. Just be yourselves and keep America happy with your down to earth personalities. The viewers really like to connect to normal people. It will be a little while before you get to the studio. After that, we will show you to the couch so you can sit down during the commercial breaks. For now, just relax and let the makeup crew do their thing."

"Thanks so much. It's nice to meet you too," Trinity said.

Juday left and they were waiting for the makeup artists to come in. Every other moment, someone would walk by and peek in to say hello. Trinity said hello to one man in particular.

"Do you know who that was?" Trinity asked Tom.

"No, who was he?"

"That was the past Federal Reserve Chairman! That is unbelievable! He must be on the show today."

Then another person peered in and said hello.

"Oh, my, I can't believe the creator of the *Medieval* series is on the show today. They really have some big names here," Elisabeth said.

Every few minutes, a different person would pop in to greet them. Juday came back to ask them how they were doing. They replied that they were doing fine and that they were really impressed with the caliber of people on the show.

Juday chuckled lightly and said, "I have been trying to keep them out of here, but everyone

334

is drawn to you this morning because they all know who you are. You are the biggest hit right now and the air is buzzing since we announced you would be on the show. This is a blockbuster and when we ran the promotional clips last night, the ratings went through the roof! We saw a spike in digital recording device and Internet usage of people recording this show. The other people may be famous, but everyone is waiting for your segment."

"Oh, wow, really?" Trinity managed.

"Yes, this is an amazing moment for our show," Juday said. Just then, she got a call on her phone and had to step out for a bit.

The makeup artist came in and helped them look their best. It was when the makeup was being finished on Edward when Juday came in once more.

"We are almost ready. We need to get to the wings of the studio to get mic'd up and ready to be seated on the couch for the show," Juday said.

They walked along the hallway to a larger room where they could see all the cameras filming a live interview. A technician pointed to a sign that said "Quiet, Please, Show in Progress."

Edward could see the control room with people moving all around and getting things just right for all the cameras. The producer was holding some papers and talking into his headset. As each camera would change position, the light on the top of the camera would indicate the live feed. They waited patiently as the interview went on. Juday motioned to them to get ready as the crew helped them get fitted for their microphones. It was almost time to go on.

Chapter 36 Interview

The host wrapped up the interview and told the television audience to stay tuned, because the next guests were the ones everyone was waiting for. They were the ones behind the diamond beanie bear sensation that was sweeping across the nation and the world. They were the reason for the phenomenon that came out of nowhere.

The show faded out to commercial and the guests on the couch got up quickly. They rushed over to meet Elisabeth, Edward, Trinity, and Tom. They wanted to meet them before the television audience did.

"This is so amazing," one of the guests said. "You are the ones behind this fun and exciting adventure?"

"Yes, we are," Trinity said.

"Oh, I can't wait to hear the story on this. I will be staying around to hear every detail," another guest said.

"Ok, ok," Juday said. "They need to get ready. Everyone will have to wait. Let's get them to the couch and ready. The commercials don't last long."

The commercials were almost finished running and they could see them on the monitor. Just as the last one ended, a promotional ran, and it was the most gripping one about them. It said that the big, exclusive story was next, so just stay tuned. It was so surreal and they could feel an abnormal amount of excitement coming from everyone in the studio. They could sense the excitement was much more than normal, but somehow the crew all seemed to stay calm and relaxed.

The producer gave the interviewers the thumbs up and the number of seconds until they were live. The cameras set up their positions and the interviewer asked them if they were ready. They all said yes and the sound guy checked that their microphones were working fine. All the crew members gave the thumbs up signal around the room. Juday looked at them and gave them the thumbs up. Their big smiles thanked Juday in return.

"Ok, here we go in 3, 2, 1. We are live!" a technician said. The interviewer had the camera on him.

"Welcome back to the show! This is a big day because this morning, friends, we have the late breaking exclusive story of the diamond beanie bears right here in our studio. This is going to be a fantastic show, so get ready to meet the people responsible for the sensation that has already swept the nation and the world. We have with us today, Trinity, Tom, Elisabeth, and Edward. Good morning to you."

"Good morning to you," they replied in unison.

"It's great to be here. Thank you for having us," Trinity said.

"Let's get right to it. You are the ones who are responsible for this renewed beanie baby bear craze. So how did this all come about?"

"Well, actually, we are not completely responsible really. It was my mother who set it all up," Trinity said.

"Your mother?" the interviewer asked.

"Yes, my mom created this whole adventure and we were the ones who brought it to life."

"Ok, come on now. Your mom set this up?"

"Yes, she did, but she passed away not too long ago."

"Oh, I am sorry to hear that. What was her name?"

"Her name was Ida."

"So your mom set it up. How did you come about finding it?"

"Well, when we were going through her effects, we came across the beanie bears. We thought they were nice, but we had no idea how nice."

"So you found some beanie bears. How did you find out they were special? I understand the way this came to life was because a little girl that was admitted to the local hospital had one of these bears. She was in really bad shape and the bear gave her some help in making her better?"

"Yes," Elisabeth said. "My friend, Melody, works at the local hospital. She was showing me the new state of the art x-ray machine and she showed me a bear they had. They used the bear to calm the little ones who needed x-rays. One time, a small boy held it in the path of the scan, and it showed a diamond in it."

"Oh, so that's how the diamond came about?" the interviewer asked.

"Yeah, that was how we found out about the diamonds in them. We knew they had unique identifiers, but we didn't know about the diamonds in them until then," Elisabeth said.

"How neat!" he said. "But for right now, we need to go for a short commercial break, so let me stop you right there. We don't want our viewing audience to miss a thing! We will get more details right after this break, so don't go anywhere, we will be right back."

The cameras switched to off and the monitor showed the commercials that were running. The producer got on the intercom and asked Juday how she wanted to proceed.

"We need to keep going as long as we need to. This is a once in a lifetime show here," Juday said.

"I agree, but we need to ask the other guests if they could come back tomorrow if needed," the producer said.

Juday agreed and went to speak with the other guests about the possible delay of their interview. The studio crew prepared to resume the show after the commercials.

"Everyone, we will be live again in a few moments. Is everyone ready? Are all of you ready?" the technician asked.

"We are ready," the interviewer said.

The promotional piece showed up on the monitor again, but this time with their pictures instead of the diamond beanie bears.

"Now everyone get ready. We are back in 3, 2, 1, live!" the technician announced.

"Welcome back. We have the diamond beanie bear group on today. Let's wrap up what we know. You didn't set up the diamond bears, but your mother did. Ida, I think you said her name was?"

"Yes, my grandmother's name was Ida," Elisabeth replied softly.

Just at that moment, a butterfly came out of nowhere and landed on Elisabeth's knee. She sat very still as the butterfly waved its wings. It was a wonderful shade of yellow and blue, and it just stayed there peacefully. Everyone in the room was quiet and still for a few moments. Even the producer in the control room was stunned. A few seconds passed until the interviewer broke the silence.

"Now that is truly neat," he said. "I have no idea where a butterfly would have come from. We are indoors, as a matter of fact. This is a sight to see for you home viewers. Can the camera get a close up on that? Oh, I see they already have. Well, there you go everyone, another remarkable moment you just witnessed here. So, let's get back to how many diamond bears your grandmother sent out."

Elisabeth sat there, mesmerized, and watched as the butterfly fluttered away out of the studio, as quietly and as magnificently as it came in.

"And how many bears did she make?" the interviewer asked.

"She made two hundred of them," Tom said.

"Wow, two hundred? Are you sure of that?"

"Yes, we are very sure. You see, she documented the bears in a list that she recorded publicly in our local Recorder's Office. She also put a notice in the advertising section of the local newspaper," Trinity said.

"That is pretty neat," the interviewer said. "So you know there are two hundred and you know there are diamonds in them? What else do you know about the bears?"

"We know they all have a blue ribbon on them and some other unique features to make sure they were the only ones she made," Elisabeth said.

"How many features and what kind are you talking about? Like a code on each one?"

"Yes, for example, she put a staple in the seam along the left ear of each one. She also put a red marker around the tag edge of each one," Elisabeth continued.

"So, she was really sure to keep them authentic, wasn't she?" he asked.

"Yes, she had these markers or identifiers on each one to make sure the adventure stayed pure, I presume," Trinity said.

"So, each bear has unique markings or identifiers on them to document their authenticity, so anyone will know they are genuine?"

"Yes, that's what she did," Tom said.

"Do you have the other diamond bears? Can we call them that?"

"Oh, no, she was all about the adventure. She put the bears out all over to give everyone a chance at finding one of them," Edward said.

"That is truly fantastic. You mean, these bears are out there somewhere, like they could be on an auction site right now?"

"They could be and probably are," Tom said.

"They could be anywhere," Trinity said. "They could be at a local church bazaar, or at a resale shop. We have no idea where she put them or where she sent all of them, but we know they are out there."

"How do you know that for sure?"

"Well, the one at the hospital proves that," Trinity said.

"Oh, I guess you got me there," he said. "So, there are two hundred beanie bears with diamonds in them, out there for anyone to find?"

"Yes," Elisabeth said. "She wanted this to be fun and shared by all."

346

"Ok, so there are so many questions, but we need to take another break right now.
Everyone stay tuned in. Please stay right there and we will get to all your questions. I know you have them, because I have them too. See you back in just a few minutes," the interviewer said, and they cut to the commercials.

Chapter 37 Exit

"We are off air now," the producer said over the intercom. "Juday, you realize we are being carried by every other morning news station right now. This story is spreading like wildfire and every newspaper is treating it like breaking news. Each time more information comes out about these bears, they are flashing it across the screen. Everyone is on edge waiting for more information."

"That's excellent," Juday replied. "We can keep this interview on until the end of the show. This will be fantastic and then we can replay the interview tonight on the nightly news magazine show."

"Yes, great idea. Let's keep it going. We will be back on air here shortly. Everyone ready again? Is the camera crew ready? Is the sound crew ready? We are back in 3, 2, 1, and we are live."

"Welcome back," the interviewer said. "I can see out the window here and there are hundreds, if not thousands of you, making your way to our studios outside. I ask that you remain orderly. I know the street is narrow outside of our studio, but you can be assured, I will get the information you would like to know in due time. Alright, then, we know there are two hundred of these diamond bears out there and Ida set this whole thing up. Are these all just bears?"

"Yeah, but they are different types of bears," Elisabeth said.

"Are these the normal looking bears?"

"Yes, they were just normal beanie bears you could buy anywhere. She just added the special features for fun," Elisabeth said.

"So, Ida made these bears as an adventure that anyone could take up and it's completely random? Do you have any of the bears to show our audience?"

"Oh, yes, I have one right here," Elisabeth said as she lifted a diamond bear from her purse. The camera quickly zoomed in on it.

"Well, there you go, folks, your first look at one of the diamond bears!"

Trinity, Tom, and Edward gasped, because they didn't know Elisabeth had one with her and that she actually brought it out to show the world. They couldn't believe it. The camera stayed zoomed in on the bear for a few moments until the interviewer jumped in.

"How do you, or anyone else, know this is an authentic beanie bear with a diamond in it?"

"We think my grandma knew all about this question and could foresee there would be people who would imitate the bears to make a quick sale, so she put the identifiers on them. She also put some other unique markers on them that only one person would know about and she sent that to Lloyd's of London," Elisabeth said.

"Lloyd's of London? How would they certify the authenticity? Won't it cost them money to do that?"

"She set up an account for anyone who thinks they have an authentic bear that needs to be verified. Then the documents would be sent to the owner of the diamond bear," Trinity said.

"What if the bear they send in is not real? Who would pay for the result?"

"I think Lloyd's would require a deposit to even look at it. They would probably keep the deposit if the bear was proven to be a fake," Trinity said.

"That solves a lot. So, there is a program set up to verify and document the ongoing location or owner of the authentic diamond bears?"

"Yeah, I think she did that to discourage people from stealing the bears from the real owners. The only way to verify the authenticity is through Lloyd's. If one came up missing, they would know who the last known true owner was," Trinity said.

"Wow, that is fantastic. She really put some thought into that one didn't she?"

"Yes, she must have," Trinity replied.

"Edward, how did you get involved in all of this? I can see how Trinity, Tom, and Elisabeth did, but how about you? But before you answer, we are going to have to hold off for a few minutes until after this commercial break. Viewers, you know the procedure. We will be right back after these messages, so stay right there."

"Folks, we are at the break," the producer said. "That was great, but the show only has limited time left, so you need to get to the conclusion."

"We will get it going then," the interviewer said.

"Hey, Juday," the producer asked. "We are getting calls right now from advertisers. They want to run their commercials on tonight's evening news magazine. They know we will run the interview again tonight for the nightly audience. They are not even asking how much it will cost. They just want to be included. I haven't seen this type of interest since the early days."

"Well, I never have either, so this is going to be fun," Juday replied.

"We will be back live here shortly, so everyone get ready. Camera number three, we are going to start off with a picture of the bear that she brought. Live in 3, 2, 1, and here we go," the technician said.

"Welcome back! You see, there it is, one of the diamond bears in the flesh. Now, I am sure everyone is asking the same question I have. Have you had this bear authenticated? Wait, not just yet, I forgot, we need to let Edward tell us how he fell into all of this. Well, Edward, how did you come to be a part of this?"

"Uh, well, I was coming from England to tour America after I was involved with Ida's other adventure with the messages in the bottles. I thought it would be fun to learn about where the one I found came from. I am a distant relative to Trinity and Elisabeth, so that made it more interesting to come over to America to tour for a while."

"What? There is another adventure? That will have to wait for another show. The real question I have is whether the diamond bear you have here today has been authenticated or not?"

"No, not yet, but we will very shortly so we can start the prominence on this one," Elisabeth said.

"So, we know there are two hundred bears out there and people can get them verified and the ownership documented. What do you four intend to do now, after this show?"

"Well, that is a good question," Tom said. "As we got involved in this adventure, we struggled with it ourselves. We knew how crazy this might get, but we never thought we would end up on national television doing an interview. We knew it was going to get wild. Ida knew it might come to this, so she wrote a diary or journal of sorts. We found it. She made her wishes known in the diary that we are to have ten of these diamond bears auctioned off for charity. Christie's will be conducting it right there in our hometown. Ida hoped it would bring some tourism there. She wanted people to know about the town she knew and was so happy to have lived in."

"Oh, so there you four go again. Out of nowhere you drop this news on America. You are going to have an auction of ten bears for anyone to be able to buy and you are going to give the proceeds to charity? This Ida was one great woman wasn't she?"

"Yes, she sure was," Elisabeth said.

"Now we know, if you don't have one or you didn't find one, everyone still has a chance to get one, and all the proceeds will go to charity. This is amazing. I can't say it enough. I think this is way more than any of us expected when we scheduled you on the show. There you have it, America, you heard it here first. We would like to continue on, but we have run out of time for the show. The rest will have to be left to another time. Thanks for watching and keep up the smile on the *Good Morning Friends* show!"

"Great show, everyone! That was amazing," the producer said. "This is going to be a time everyone will remember well. Enjoy it and have a great day."

Juday helped them get their microphones off and hurried them down the hallway to a stairwell opposite the one they came up on. She stopped at the end of the hall and asked them if they had everything they brought.

"Yes, we do," Tom said. "Why?"

"We never expected the tremendous response we just got. You saw all the throngs of people outside waiting for the end of the show. There is no way we can let you try to get through that mob, but we got really lucky. We just got a call from a wealthy benefactor who was so touched by your story that he pledged to pay your costs to get you back home safely, privately, and incognito. We have our corporate private jet taxied up for you. It will take you home to your local airport, so you can bypass all the hype that is bearing down on you now. We have it set up for you to be driven to the private airport in a black car. We have all your effects in the car right now, so you are ready to go to the airport. Is that alright with you?" Juday said.

"Yes, of course. You are the best," Tom replied.

"We are so grateful for all you have done for us and Ida's adventure," Trinity said.

"Yeah, thanks a lot," Elisabeth said.

"It was great to meet you," Edward said.

"You are so very welcome," Juday replied. "If you want to come back on, just give me a call."

"You have a deal," Tom said.

Juday led them down the rear stairwell. She hoped that by using the maintenance stairway, the utilitarian nature of its appearance would not draw attention to them. When she opened the door to the alley, she saw the non-descript car that waited to pick them up. They all climbed into an extremely dark car with tinted windows. Juday closed the door for them. She glanced around to be sure they weren't spotted, went back into the building, and closed the door quickly. The car drove off down the road to the main street. It turned down the next street until they came to a light. As they were stopped at the light, they could see down the street to the front of the studio. There were hundreds, if not thousands of people, waiting around to catch a glimpse of them. Little did they know they had all slipped away unnoticed.

Tom smiled widely and gave the thumbs up to Trinity. He was happy that they made it cleanly out. The ride to the airport was quick and easy, as it seemed they were always driving the opposite direction of the heavy traffic. They were headed to the small, private airport, to board the corporate jet, to go back home.

Chapter 38 Cruiser

They arrived in short order. The car pulled into a small, gated entrance and onto the tarmac, where there was a shiny, clean twin jet private plane. It was waiting for them with the stairway down. The car parked right at the bottom of the stairs, so they all hopped out and began the ascent up to the jet. Their luggage was loaded quickly and before they knew it, they were taxiing along the runway for lift off.

The takeoff was so quick they could hardly catch their breath. The plane was very quiet, but didn't fly as smoothly as the large commercial jets. It seemed a lot faster though, and they could watch the ground pass under them as they made their way back to LaPorte.

Tom and Trinity dozed off right away. Elisabeth and Edward spent the whole time talking about the whirlwind they were on. It was amazing to discuss and would be completely unbelievable if they had not just experienced it.

It wasn't but a few minutes until they were getting into Indiana airspace. Trinity nudged Tom awake and asked him if he could call his friend to have a deputy meet them at the airport. She wanted to make sure they could get back to the cabin safely, just in case there might be people waiting for them. After all the publicity at the studio, people would surely be waiting for them at home, even if they didn't know they were not flying a commercial airline.

Tom was a little groggy, but he agreed, and dialed his phone to call his friend.

"Hello?"

"Yes, this is Tom."

"Tom, I see you had quite a day today. This place is crazy. There are people all around your house. I try to keep them away, but they keep driving up and down the road."

"Well, I can't thank you enough, but we need to know if you can set up another deputy to pick us up at the city airport and get us to the cabin. You see we were given a private jet to take us home after the whole explosion of attention we got on the television show."

"I see your point. You do need someone to help you get back safely."

"Yes, I think we do."

"Not a problem, I can arrange that, but it will not be a marked car, except for the deputy plate."

"Thanks so much. I owe you big time now."

"Oh, it's my pleasure. I could get an interview out of this," he laughed.

"You probably could," Tom said. "We will be landing in about forty-five minutes."

"Alright, I will have someone there for you."

"Ok, thanks," Tom said and pushed the end button on his phone.

The planed cruised to a landing effortlessly on the small runway and taxied to an area behind a large hangar. The plane stairs opened up and each of them walked down. Tom got out first and he waved hello to the deputy that was waiting next his car by the hangar.

"Oh, thank goodness," Trinity said. "We have a quiet way to get back to the cabin now."

Tom walked over and shook his hand to say thanks for helping out. The deputy put their things in the trunk and they all got into the cruiser. The plane was already taxiing off to the runway to depart as they made their way out onto the state highway to go north.

They were driving back towards town and the deputy was talking to Tom about their trip. Tom wanted to make sure he kept their location secret until they ironed out the details of the auction. The deputy was happy to help them out. He would make sure no one would know where they were, so he would take a winding path back after he dropped them off.

Trinity was in the back seat and leaned forward to ask Tom if they could stop at the local neighborhood store. She needed to pick up some things and maybe some fresh steaks from the butcher. Tom asked her if that was a good idea since someone might notice them after they had been on the television show.

"Oh, I would think they might notice us at the large grocery store, but not the neighborhood store," Trinity said.

"No one would be expecting you to show up there," the deputy said. "Besides, you could be in and out in a quick second."

"Yeah, that is what I was thinking," Trinity said.

"I guess you could be right," Tom said.

"Ooh, I can smell the steaks on the grill right now!" Edward said smiling.

The deputy turned down Eighteenth Street and then went north on I Street to the small, neighborhood grocery store. The were no cars in the parking lot, so they hurried into the store, picked out the items they needed, paid, and made their way to the exit. Tom pushed the store front door to leave and at the same time another older gentleman was walking in.

"Oh, hello," Tom said, startled.

"Oh, hello," the gentleman replied.

Trinity stood behind Tom and they were both stuck in their tracks. The deputy opened the car door and was going to move to them like a quick jackrabbit, when Tom motioned to him to hold off.

The gentleman looked at them curiously for a moment, like he was waiting for them to move out of the way, so he could go into the store. Just then the gentleman's expression changed and his face lit up.

"Hey, are you the same people with those fancy diamond bears on TV the other morning?" he asked.

Trinity squeezed Tom's arm and Tom looked back at her.

"Oh no, that is not us, but I did hear about that," he replied quickly.

"Well, you know us old county surveyors, sometimes we remember things differently, but you sure do look like the people on that *Good Morning Friends* show," he quipped.

366

"Thanks, but if we were on that show yesterday, with all the hoopla surrounding it, we would surely be living large right now, instead of picking up some steaks for grilling tonight," Edward said, as he was pushing Trinity and Tom out the door towards the cruiser.

"Yeah, I guess you're right. I hope you left some steaks for me!" the gentleman replied humorously.

"You got it, and some good ones are still left," Tom said, and they hurriedly got into the cruiser and drove away in haste.

"That went well. I don't think anyone even knew we were with a deputy," Elisabeth said.

"Yeah, it's good this car is only one color. It makes it more incognito. You see, we just started getting these one color cars recently. It is supposed to save money for the county," the deputy said smiling.

They went through town with nary a second look from anyone. As they were traveling on the east side of town, the scanner in the cruiser crackled. It was another deputy mic'ing up his radio.

"Station, this is Deputy Michaels. I am going to be out directing traffic around the beanie subdivision for a little while. It is congested and I am going to get people moving along, so the residents can get in and out."

"Ten-four, we will note it on the call list," the dispatcher said.

"Ten-four," the deputy answered.

"Wow, are you kidding me?" Elisabeth said. "Did I hear what I think I heard?"

"Yes," the deputy said. "Everything around here has been taken over by the diamond beanie bear frenzy. They all want to know about the bears."

"So they are driving around our subdivision?" Trinity asked.

"Yes, your road is a virtual traffic jam. It's a good thing your deputy friend is there to keep them moving along," the deputy said.

368

"He is great. I will owe him big time," Tom said.

"You sure will, but I think he might really like the notoriety anyway," the deputy replied.

"You are probably right," Tom said.

"I know how important it is to keep your new location under wraps, so they put me on traffic duty where everyone thinks you will show up," the deputy said.

They drove to the cottage at the lake and the deputy helped them get their things into the house. Tom thanked him and he drove back to town in a wandering pattern to make sure no one wised up to the fact that they were back in town and staying up north.

Chapter 39 Charity

"Alright everyone, we need to get the plan together for the auction as soon as possible. We have to get this all quieted down," Tom said.

"That would be a good idea," Trinity and Edward replied simultaneously.

"We need to get ahold of Christie's to set up the date and have them make all the arrangements for the venue. I figured the civic center would be great. It will probably fill up, but it will be good for the town's economy," Tom said.

"I agree, that would be a good place," Elisabeth said.

"We need to make sure we have the charities picked out for the auction proceeds," Trinity said.

"Yes, we need to find some charities that give a person a hand up, not a hand out," Tom said.

"I agree with that," Edward said. "It is better to teach someone to fish, than give them a fish. If you teach someone to fish, they eat for a lifetime."

"I do not want to be the story about giving a charity some money and watching it get squandered," Tom said.

"Oh, yeah, I saw an article on charities a few months ago. It said to look into the overhead or administrative costs of the charities, because you want the funds to go to people who actually need the help, and not to the people running the charity making large salaries," Elisabeth said.

"Those are good ideas. Edward, why don't you help Tom on the Internet to research charities? Elisabeth and I will get Christie's set up," Trinity said.

"Ok, that sounds good," Edward replied.

They researched the charities and found contacts for three they wanted to be the recipients of the auction proceeds. Elisabeth found the contact for Christie's and emailed them a request. She gave them Trinity's phone number and her email address.

Tom was getting the grill running and Trinity was preparing some side dishes for a late afternoon meal. Elisabeth was searching the Internet and her social site when she heard Trinity's phone ring. She knew exactly who it was without looking, but could not believe it was that fast. She grabbed Trinity's phone and answered.

"Hello?"

"Hello, this is a representative from Christie's inquiring about an email we just received. We are following up on every email and if this is real, we need to discuss some things."

"Oh, hello, this is Elisabeth. I left you the email for my mom, but I can help you."

"Well, first we need to verify you are the same people that were on the morning show. Can you tell me who the person was that set up your interview on the show? I will need her phone number for verification too. We have gotten a lot of false leads from people trying to get us to run an auction for them using these supposed diamond beanie bears they saw on television."

"Yes, I understand. Let me get my phone so I can give you Juday's number."

"You just got the first question right," the representative said.

Elisabeth looked at her phone and reviewed the recent numbers. She read Juday's number to the representative, who held quiet for a moment.

"I am going to put you on speaker phone," the representative said. "Can you hear us?"

"Yes, I can hear you."

"I have with me here, the vice president of marketing, and our field staff. We would be happy to host your auction for you, if you should decide to do business with us."

"Oh, good, let me get my mom. She needs to speak with you to get this going. Hold on for a minute."

Elisabeth went into the kitchen and told her mom she needed to talk to Christie's. Trinity was finishing up the cooking, so she washed her hands, and grabbed the phone from Elisabeth.

"Hello, this is Trinity."

"Hello there, we need to go over some details about the auction. We would like to host it for you. Do you have a place you were thinking of holding the auction at?"

"Yes, we would like to have it here in town at the civic center."

"Is that a private venue?"

"No, it is owned by the city, so you could call them tomorrow and see what their schedule is."

"We can do that. How about the format of the auction? Would you want it in person, online, by telephone, all of the above, or a combination of those?"

"Oh, I think we want everyone to have a chance to bid on the diamond bears," Trinity said.

"We can get this all taken care of in the next few days. What we need you to do, as soon as possible, is to have the diamond bears you are going to auction off sent out for verification. We will need to get the certificates of authenticity.

Then we will make arrangements to meet with you somewhere to go over the finalized plans for the auction."

"Alright, thank you," Trinity said. "If you need me sooner, please call me at this number or email me. I will get right back with you."

"Thank you, Trinity, for choosing us to have this auction. We are all extremely excited over here."

"Oh, we are too," Trinity said.

"We will be in touch soon. Goodbye for now."

Trinity hung up the phone and went to the kitchen. Edward and Elisabeth had the table set and Tom brought the grilled steaks in to eat. They sat at the table and discussed the upcoming auction and how they needed to get things in motion.

Elisabeth was going to get the beanie bears and ship them by next day air to Lloyd's for verification and then shipped back to the cottage. Edward was going to scout out a way to get around town and get things ready without being noticed. Tom and Trinity were going to set up the auction and charity details.

They all slept well that night, as the day was extremely long, and they could sense that completeness was soon to come.

Chapter 40 Auction

Christie's called back several times to work out some more details. They had been able to book the civic center within ten days and were taking care of all the logistic details. Tom had been on the phone and also used email to secure all the necessary contacts for the auction proceeds. Elisabeth had sent out the bears and would receive them in about four days. Edward handled all the transportation plans.

Each day the energy of anticipation around the town grew. A few days later, Christie's made a press release about the upcoming auction. The time and place was set and the entire town was getting ready for the huge event.

The tenth day had finally arrived, and the town was a beehive of activity. Every hotel for miles around was booked solid and every television station was set up outside of the civic center. The vans with satellite dishes on them abounded every street surrounding the place of the event.

The people were lined up for days prior to the auction and a virtual tent city invaded every open space downtown. It was an amazing sight. The impact on the small town was something never seen before and maybe never to be seen again. The citizens were overjoyed to have all the attention, but were also longing for the quiet days when things went along like clockwork each day.

The traffic would get busy in the morning and late afternoon when people were coming and going from work. The courthouse would bustle with the normal flow of people taking care of their business and days would pass just like a finely tuned machine. The last few days had been near chaos, with the restaurants filled to capacity, and delivery trucks sometimes arriving twice a day with supplies for the grocery stores.

There was nary a place to park anywhere and the homes in town were renting out parking spaces for people who would come into town to take a tour. The courthouse had a waiting line with special times for guided tours. The libraries were at safety capacities and each person had to wait patiently to review the verification documents that were held there. The resale shops were holding open houses as everyone around town had already bought any beanie bear that had been for sale. It was controlled chaos just working its way up to the auction day.

The day was a bright, sunny, cold morning and the steady hum of all the backup power generators filled the air. Vendors from all over were brought in to create a fair-like atmosphere around the center. Everyone waited with anticipation until the doors opened. Each person had already bought tickets for the reserved seating and an adequate window of time was allowed to give everyone a chance to get to their seats for the auction. It was a splendid time around the civic center and each person found their seat in an orderly fashion. Christie's spared no expense in decorating the center with lavish tapestries and jumbotrons so that everyone inside and outside could watch the auction.

Edward, Elisabeth, Trinity, and Tom all arrived through the VIP entrance in the back of the building. They drove Ida's car and it was nondescript, so no one paid attention to them when they pulled into the reserved parking space in the back.

The auctioneer was behind the stage sets and could see the audience was ready. She looked over to the crew and they gave her the thumbs up. The technicians running the phone bank and the computers connected to the Internet gave the thumbs up. It was exactly the time published on the promotional material and the auctioneer walked out to the podium. She received a standing ovation and a hearty round of applause. The whole building roared to life and it took several minutes before everyone sat down.

The auctioneer had never been in a situation quite like this, but she could feel the warm and welcoming sense of home everywhere in the building. She adjusted the microphone one more time and then smiled widely to welcome everyone to the auction.

"We are glad everyone could join us here, on the telephone and online. We are pleased to be the auction house chosen to provide you with this once in a lifetime sale of magical proportions. We have with us tonight, ten verified and authenticated diamond beanie babies. The winning bidder will get the documents to secure their prominence as the new owner. We also have with us here tonight, the people who brought to light the diamond beanie bears. They have chosen the charities the proceeds will go to. At the end of the auction, we will post those on the newly created diamond beanie website. Now we do have a special announcement to tell you and the originators of the diamond beanie bears. This is a surprise and everyone will be hearing this for the first time. We are pleased to inform everyone we have an anonymous donor, who has agreed to match the proceeds from the auctions, dollar for dollar. So if you are willing to bid on any bear, please keep in mind, the higher the final bid, the greater the match will be for the charities chosen. We will be starting out with, appropriately enough, the beginning bear. This bear is authenticated and will go the highest bidder today. Let's start the bidding."

As the auction started fast and furiously, the crowd bid higher and there seemed to be a battle between the in-house crowd, the phone-in bidders, and the Internet bidders. It was a sight to see as the price went from one hundred dollars, to ten thousand dollars, to nearly one hundred thousand dollars. When the gavel came down on the first bear, the tone was set. This was going to exceed any monetary estimate even Christie's could imagine.

The news crews were running the live feed in record format. Even the announcers for the news crews could barely contain themselves when the bids shattered the previous limits. The crowd was amazed and the energy in the building was growing greater every moment. The auctioneer was feeding off the energy and each bear sold brought on a deafening round of applause as soon as the gavel went down.

The moments were filled with joy and each winning bidder had grasped a piece of history. Everyone knew the ten specially chosen bears to be auctioned off were not the only ones out there, but they also knew those ten would be the most valuable of the two hundred placed into circulation. The auction went exactly as scheduled and ended in perfect time, just as the program stated. As the last one sold, the gavel came down to enormous applause. The auctioneer stood at the podium with one final announcement.

"I would like to thank everyone for coming and participating in this truly amazing moment in time. It brings warmth to my heart to know all the good we have all done today. It will surely help people from every walk of life to make their life a little better. We have one more item to release today, before you go out to find the diamond bears hiding out there. They are surely hidden gems, wherever they may be. We are happy to tell you we have a report from Lloyd's stating they have verified forty-four diamond beanies as of today. Those combined with those ten sold today, makes a total of fifty-four diamond beanies that have been found so far. The big announcement is that there are still one hundred and fifty-six still unaccounted for, so we wish everyone the best of luck in finding them. Who knows where they will turn up, but please enjoy the adventure in locating them. You might even run into me during your hunt." An enthusiastic round of applause went up again, and the auctioneer could only stand there and smile graciously until the hoopla calmed. "Thank you again and good luck to everyone. God bless!"

The hall emptied in the most unbelievable orderly fashion. In a matter of a few hours, the main street in town was quiet again. The masses of people seemed to slip away into the night, just as quietly as they had arrived. The sense of relief coming from all the residents was palpable. Later in the evening, the main street was just as empty as it had been a few weeks earlier.

Edward drove Elisabeth, Trinity, and Tom back to their house and dropped them off. They were all at home enjoying the relief the auction had brought. A few days later, Edward stopped by. He thanked them for all they had done for him and that they made him feel at home when he first came to America. He handed Trinity the keys to Ida's house and thanked her for everything she had done. He was moving into an apartment near the university campus and would be going to school for his master's degree in historical technology. He thanked Tom for all his solid advice. He thanked Elisabeth for all the fun they had together and told her he would probably see her on campus.

"Ok, Edward, I will see you at the Tricycle," she said.

"Yeah, ok," he replied, wondering what in the world that meant.

It was a few weeks later and the university campus was bustling with a young, vibrant crowd of students. Most of them were heading for their cars to go home and Edward was walking by the parking lot toward his new apartment. As he walked through the lot, he thought he saw Elisabeth's car parked near the pine trees. He went over to the car and was happy to see that it was her. She was leaving for the day. When she saw Edward, her face lit up, and she rolled her window down to call to him.

"Edward! Hello!"

"Hey, Elisabeth, it's great to see you! How is your semester going?"

"Oh, it's going well, you know. I have been here long enough to know the ropes."

"Yes, it does take a little time to learn the ins and outs of the campus. Well, it is really good to see you."

"Yes, you too!"

387

"Oh, wait, I figured out what you were talking about when you said you would see me at the Tricycle. Were you talking about the big Tricycle out here?"

"Yeah, you got it."

"Yes, the Tres Bon Tricycle. The one the present county surveyor helped make," he said and smiled.

"What is with the Tres Bon thing?"

"Oh, yeah, like you don't know," Edward said. "You know, Tres Bon Medal."

He looked at her sternly, but she just looked back at him and grinned.

"Oh, you are not going to draw me into that one! Tres Bon Medal," she repeated. "You know better than that."

Elisabeth put her car in gear and pulled away, leaving Edward standing there with a quizzical look on his face.

NCPL
Morocco Community Library
205 S. West Street
P O Box 87
Morocco, IN 47963

13119574R00237

Made in the USA
San Bernardino, CA
09 July 2014